# BAD BEST FRIEND

# BAD BEST FRIEND

### RACHEL VAIL

VIKING

VIKING
An imprint of Penguin Random House LLC, New York

First published in the United States of America by Viking,
an imprint of Penguin Random House LLC, 2020

Visit us online at penguinrandomhouse.com

LIBRARY OF CONGRESS CATALOGING-IN-PUBLICATION DATA IS AVAILABLE
ISBN 9780451479457

Printed in the USA

10   9   8   7   6   5   4   3   2   1

To my brother, Jon, with love.
I am your friend, and your biggest fan,
forever.

# BAD BEST FRIEND

# 1

"EVERYBODY STAND NEXT to your best friend," the gym teacher said.

I bumped Ava's shoulder with mine.

We were already standing next to each other, of course.

We've been best friends since third grade, basically since the day she moved here. No. A few weeks after. Still, nearly forever. It's not like we were making a big, momentous decision right there in front of the entire eighth grade. Everybody knows Ava and I are best friends.

So I wasn't worried or anything. Knowing, hundred percent, that you can choose her, and that your best friend will of course choose you right back, right away, in front of everybody, no hesitation? Best feeling in the world.

But Ava didn't bump me back.

I rolled my eyes at Ava and whispered, "We're not even supposed to have best friends, I thought."

It's a rule at Snug Island Primary School: *We Are All Friends*

*Here!* There's a poster saying that at the entrance. Ava and I make fun of how fake it is. *Come on in and start your day with a lie, kids!* We walk under those words literally every day: *We Are All Friends Here!* The only SIPS teacher who'd ever admit it's not exactly true, that we're maybe not all friends, not all equal friends, don't even necessarily like each other all that much? It *would be* Ms. Andry, the ancient gym teacher. She's so over it, no time for that politically correct fakery. Ava and I love how fully fried Ms. Andry is.

Ava wasn't saying anything back to me.

She was looking at her sneakers.

I looked at her sneakers too.

That's why I saw her sneakers step-together-step away from me.

Toward Britney.

I smiled at Ava. My mom says, *Smiles, sunshine, and a quick cleanup make everything better!* "Why is Ms. Andry always so extra?" I whispered to Ava.

Ava always says, *Why is Ms. Andry so extra?*

This time, Ava didn't say anything.

"I mean, what's even her actual plan?" I whispered.

Ava forced out a little one-ha laugh. But she still wouldn't look at me.

Ms. Andry pointed her bony witch finger right at me. "You!" she said.

*Do not pee in your pants, Niki*, I told myself.

"Who are you with?" she barked at me.

I was very busy not peeing in my pants so did not have

a chance to answer evil Ms. Andry at that time.

"Who's your person?" Ms. Andry barked at Ava, having realized I was worthless.

"Britney," Ava said.

"Britney? That's somebody's *name*?" Ms. Andry asked. "Which one is Britney?"

Ava pointed her thumb at, well, Britney.

Everybody knows Britney. Britney, Isabel, and Madeleine. They're the Squad. Even Ms. Andry had to know that.

Britney leaned toward Ava, my best friend, and whispered into her ear. Ava's heart-shaped mouth puckered into a smile.

"So who's yours?" Ms. Andry asked me. Trying again.

I was watching Ava. She was whispering something back to Britney. The two of them flicked their eyes toward me. When they saw I was watching them, they turned quickly away, in unison.

"This isn't calculus, kids," Ms. Andry barked. "Just pick your best friend; I don't care who's your partner. There's an even number of you people, come on."

"What if our best friend isn't here?" Bradley asked.

"Oh, like you have a best friend," Chase said.

"Eat dirt, Chase," Bradley said. "Your best friend is your mom."

"My best friend is *your* mom!" Chase said back.

Ava and the Squad were all cracking up at the boys and their loud dissing. Bradley and Chase are best friends. They, along with Robby and Milo, are the boys who Britney, Isabel, and Madeleine hang out with. They have nothing to do with me and Ava anymore. Robby and Milo live next door to me, and we used to play together all the time, but now they glowed up and I, well, haven't.

"It doesn't matter," Ms. Andry interrupted the boys. "You two lugs can work together. Just choose a partner. Let's go. Who's left without a friend?"

I raised my hand a little, pushed it up into the air, into the concrete-air of shame weighing it down.

Across the gym, Holly Jones raised her hand too.

No. No. *You can't go backward.*

"Fine," Ms. Andry said. "You and you." She pointed at Holly Jones, and then at me. Holly walked across the gym toward me.

I kept my eyes on my feet on the high-gloss gym floor. Same sneakers as Ava's, one size bigger because my feet are disproportionately huge for my body. Same style, though: Superstars. Got them together, Ava's mom's treat. Ms. Andry was explaining the exercise we were supposed to do, something called trust falls. I didn't listen to the instructions because I couldn't hear anything but the ocean drowning me from inside my head.

Also because I didn't care.

Holly was saying something, next to me.

I don't know what, because I was very focused on not yelling, YOU ARE NOT MY BEST FRIEND. AVA IS MY BEST FRIEND. WHAT IS HAPPENING.

I gritted my teeth against it and tried to hear what Holly was saying.

"Who does she think she is, Noah?" Holly whispered out of the side of her mouth.

"What?" I managed. "Noah who?" Ugh, just what I needed was to hear about some cousin of Holly's named Noah, or some kid named Noah she knew from some retreat her weird, crunchy hippie family went on or something. *I NEED TO TALK TO AVA*, I was thinking. *I NEED TO SORT THIS OUT. I AM NOT BEST FRIENDS WITH YOU ANYMORE, HOLLY.*

"Noah! You know, Noah, loading up the ark?" Holly asked.

"I'm not religious," I said.

"Me either," Holly whispered. "As you know! But you know, like, two by two?"

"Right," I said. Right, except me. Like the unchosen llama or hippopotamus or squirrel, I was suddenly and publicly alone.

Paired with this, what, porcupine? Or, to be fair, koala. Whatever, something slightly exotic and sweet. But not two of a kind with me *at all*.

What happened to the animals stranded alone like that on the ground in front of the ark? The left-out animals, the third ones? I'd never thought about them before. Did they slink away, or did they strike?

If you're the third lion, you're dead.

Worse than dead, being the third lion, the extra elephant: condemned to the rising flood. Pre-dead, and knowing it.

Knowing, as you watch the other animals go two by two,

that there'd be no place for you inside the ark, no safety. That this is your fate, the end of the line for you. You'd just have to stand there in the drizzle. Alone, abandoned. An unchosen elephant alongside the third koala, maybe, but not half a pair, so basically alone. A random. Watching the two elephants who'd just been right beside you, one of them the one you'd expected to be your partner, as they swish their tails (ponytails) behind them in self-satisfied unison, going giggling up the gangplank onto the ark.

Feeling the floodwaters rise around your sagging ankles.

Ava was catching Britney. Britney was falling, backward, gracefully, toward Ava. *Drop her*, I wished horribly at them. My mom thinks I am nice. I am obviously not.

The two of them were laughing. Shrieking, just like Madeleine and Isabel, who were also falling backward at each other, taking turns.

I looked full-on at Holly for the first time, with her thick blue-framed glasses, her short cloud of black hair. She was looking back at me. Her face was serious, her mouth a straight line.

*Worse than alone*, I thought at her sweet, solemn face.

She turned around. I held out my arms for her to fall backward toward me. I felt her pouf of weight hit my arms, and stumbled to not drop her. I succeeded, but it was close.

She was light.

She stood up and faced me again without smiling. "Your turn," she said.

"No, thanks," I said.

"You can trust me," she said. Her eyes are huge and gray, like a manga drawing.

I turned my back to her.

I let myself fall, but not because I trusted Holly. How could I?

Her. Anybody.

I let myself fall backward because who even cares.

She caught me.

Whatever.

It's not like falling flat on the floor would have made my day worse.

# 2

LUNCH IS RIGHT after gym, but Ava didn't wait for me by our stuff. I hung back a few seconds to see if she would. Maybe Britney had grabbed Ava's arm before I bumped her shoulder, I told myself. Ava and Britney had been talking more lately—maybe Ava, being kind, felt bad for Britney being the third wheel in her friend group? Maybe Ava felt pulled, in that moment, and was trying to be nice and generous to the, well, the most popular girl in the entire grade, whatever, fine, that doesn't make sense but I just hung back a sec because who knows, maybe Ava would be like, *Come on, Niki, why are you always so slow?* And then what had just happened to me, being abandoned in gym class right in front of the entire grade, would have not happened.

Or at least would be in the past.

Would be explainable in ways I couldn't know yet, being still in the moment.

Like the curvature of the earth something something or

whatever nonsense the science teacher had been spouting the period before my life went off a freaking cliff.

But no.

Ava grabbed her stuff and hurried to catch up to the Squad.

I wasn't about to follow along after them.

And anyway, who was I supposed to sit with? I sit with Ava.

I walked the forty-seven miles across the gym to pick up my stuff and then I just stood there holding it for a minute.

"What's wrong with you?" Ms. Andry barked at me. She's the first teacher I've ever been taller than.

"Good question," I said.

"I don't actually care," Ms. Andry said. "You just have to leave so I can lock the door."

"Right," I said. I walked out of the gym and stood there while she locked the door behind us.

"You lost?" Ms. Andry asked.

"Deeply," I said.

"Well," she said. "Cope."

Not sure why that gave me life enough to smile, watching Ms. Andry's tiny hunched back as she walked away. If I ever admitted to my mom that I was feeling lost, wow, she'd talk me to death. She'd probe why, and want to brainstorm strategies with me for how to manage my feelings and what Ava might be going through to cause her to hurt me. My mom is the nicest person I've ever met. I was so glad she wasn't seeing me right then. She has enough to deal with.

Instead of going to the cafeteria, I went to the library. It's supposed to be quiet in there. So nobody would be able to talk to me, and I could have a few minutes to pull myself together, talk myself out of how bad I felt.

I sat down at one of the tables in front and tried to start my homework, at least be productive. But then, instead, I put my head down on my notebook and closed my eyes. I didn't want to see that the only other eighth grader in the library was Holly Jones, the kid I dumped as a friend back in third grade, along with Milo and Robby, because Ava was my *best friend*. *Why are you leaving me out?* Ava would ask anytime I tried to play with Holly, too. Or, *Why is she always trying to play with us?* Or, when I played with Milo and Robby: *You don't like BOYS, do you?*

It had felt stressful, trying to explain myself to Ava, and I didn't want to hurt her feelings, which I knew were fragile despite her outward feisty boldness. But more than that, it was more fun to play with Ava than anyone else anyway. I felt guilty that Holly looked confused and sad that I stopped playing with her, but it's not like we were officially *best* friends—that wasn't even a thing at that point. Plus, friend groups change, sometimes, Mom said. She and Ava's mom, Samantha, and Ava and I—we were a tight group pretty quickly. And at school everybody wanted to play with Ava, but she always told them all I was her best friend. I stopped looking at Holly's sad gray eyes when Ava said, *Niki's my best friend*, and just let myself enjoy it. Anyway, Holly had other friends, like Nadine and Beth; it's not like I abandoned her in an empty field.

If Holly was a porcupine getting onto Noah's ark, now, though, my only chance to save myself was to be her porcupine partner.

I glanced up at her, shelving books off the cart, smiling to herself, wonky, nerdy, wholesome.

No thanks, universe. No.

I'll take the storm.

# 3

I GOT OUT of eighth period as fast as I could and dashed to my locker. I wasn't waiting around for Ava this time. Whatever was going on with her, she could find me when she was ready. Sometimes she gets like this, I reminded myself. It always ends faster if I don't chase after her.

*Ava's fragile.*

I shoved my stuff into my backpack, grabbed my scooter, and was out the door before the hallway even filled up. Ava complains I'm slow sometimes? I'm not. Not always.

I scooted home fast. Ava and I like scooters, not bikes like the Squad. What was she planning to do, scoot beside them as they rode their bikes?

It was the wind in my eyes making tears stream out, I lied to myself.

Just the wind.

I went straight up to my room, followed by our dog, Fumble, and closed the door behind us. Mom didn't need to see me with red eyes. Fumble wandered around in a circle a couple of times and ended up back where he'd started. Exhausted by the journey, he flopped down for a rest.

I floofed his ears.

I checked my phone. Nothing.

**You okay?** I texted Ava.

Send.

Whatever.

Not overthinking it—I reached out. Now it's her turn to respond, if she wants to.

*If she wants to?* WE ARE BEST FRIENDS.

"Niki?" Mom yelled up the stairs.

"Yeah?"

"You ready?"

"For what?"

"Danny's Little League game, remember?"

I flopped down on my bed.

My brother, Danny, is almost nine, in fourth grade. He has been in Little League since kindergarten. My mom goes to every one of his games, and my dad to most. Danny has never hit the ball—I don't mean never got a home run or he's not the star of his team; he has never swung the bat at the ball, not once. He is the worst Little Leaguer in the history of Little League. I was not what you'd call an asset to my team, honestly, but at least I quit. Danny plays fall ball and spring ball. My parents think it will help him improve. They both played all the sports.

I asked him this summer if he likes Little League. He shrugged. He was watching TV at the time.

I like scooting, jumping on beds, making up my own games, cutting together mash-ups of politicians saying *ummm* on the news. Luckily for me I make my parents laugh, and my brother makes them worry; the combination gets me out of a lot of pressure.

Knock on my door.

Mom hates when I close it all the way.

"Come in," I said.

Mom opened it partway and leaned against the doorframe, one foot on top of the other. She's very fit. She and Ava's mom, Samantha, go running, three miles, every morning together, and a longer run on Saturdays. They're best friends too.

"It means so much to Danny when you come," Mom whispered.

"I have to read this whole book," I lied.

"Bring it," she said. "Come on, keep me company. I have no friends among the moms on the team this year."

"Sure," I said. Meaning, sarcastically, sure she has no friends. She has all the friends. Everybody likes her. She grew up on this rock and is friends with pretty much everybody on it. But that's not how she took it.

"Oh goodie!" she said, beaming her smile at me. "Yay! Quick, quick, let's go. I have to get Danny to put on his uniform and for some reason . . ."

"Cut out the tag," I suggested, getting off my bed.

Danny hates tags in his clothes.

"You're a genius!" Mom yelled. "You're, like, the Danny

Whisperer. Grab the box of doughnuts, will you, Niki? On the counter!"

I followed her down the stairs, tucking my phone into my pocket as I went.

I picked up the box of doughnuts Mom had bought for Danny's team and went to sit in the car. Back seat. Old rule: if we're both in the car, we both sit in the back, so it's fair. Even though I am almost five years older.

I put the box of doughnuts in the front seat and took out my phone to play a game on it while I waited.

A text.

From Ava. Phew.

**Ayuh.**

That's all she said. She always makes fun of how Mainers say *ayuh* instead of *yeah*. She's lived here since she was seven. She still isn't a Mainer, not really, she says. Everybody says.

Was that *Ayuh* making fun of *me*? I don't say that. I don't think I do, anyway.

Mom and Danny got into the car. Danny had his shoes in his hands, and half a tuna sandwich balanced precariously on top of them.

I opened my window as soon as Mom turned the car on.

"Can you close that?" Mom asked.

"His sandwich smells."

"No commenting on other people's food choices!" Danny yelled, with tuna sandwich bits falling out of his mouth and onto his shoes and sweatshirt and whatever else he was holding.

I turned away.

"Just hurry and finish, Danny," Mom said. "Niki, please?"

I closed my window.

"You're the finest kind," Mom said, catching my eyes in the rearview.

I smiled but didn't say it back.

# 4

I SAT IN the stands next to my mother, looking out at the ocean, wondering if anybody in Little League has ever hit a ball that far. Obviously not the fourth graders, especially Danny. He walks or strikes out, depending entirely on the pitcher. My butt was already starting to itch from sitting on the wood bleachers and we were only three innings in.

Mom was chatting happily with all the other parents. Of course.

Madeleine's mom was one of them, since Madeleine's sister, Margot, is the pitcher on Danny's team. Like Madeleine (and their mom, Marya), Margot is tiny, adorable, very athletic. The mom, Marya, said a friendly hello to me. She's always friendly and perfect, in her cute cardigans and smooth dark hair just like Madeleine's and Margot's, but was today's hello extra?

I slumped down over my book, wondering if Madeleine's mom or any of the other parents had heard what had happened to me in gym class.

Not paranoid. A fully likely possibility, honestly.

I mean, we live on an island. In the summer it's packed here, but most of the summer people left three weeks ago, after Labor Day. Not that many families live on Snug Island full-time over the winter, so it's not that huge a school. Everybody knows everybody else, and your family and your grandparents and if you were weird in kindergarten or you got dumped by your best friend fourth period today or who your mom went out with in high school if she grew up here too. (She did, my mom; Dad didn't. She went out briefly with a kid named Jerome who died of cancer a few years later. There's a plaque about him in the high school. It doesn't mention that he went to the prom with my mom on the plaque, just that he was on swim team and exemplified the values of Snug Island HS, whatever the heck those values might be. Mom says he was sweet, and smiles sadly. *It was a long time ago*, she sometimes adds.)

"What's going on?" Mom whispered at me.

"Nothing. I have to write three pages on this book I haven't read!"

A lie. I just like to read. Mom thinks I should try to be friendlier, out and about.

"Fun, fun," Mom said. She was probably in whatever the Squad was called when she was in eighth grade.

"Look, Niki! There's Madeleine and Isabel!"

I peeked. Oh, dread. They saw me, because of my mom waving at them.

"Stop," I begged Mom in a whisper.

She draped her long tan arm around my shoulders. "Everything good?"

"I just . . ."

"I know, you have to read. But friends are important too, Niki. You want to invite them over for pizza or something sometime?"

I shrugged. Madeleine and Isabel were getting off their bikes.

"Think about it—we could get a movie or something."

I don't like people to come over. My mom doesn't get that and it's not a thing I can explain to her without making her super mad about why, so I try to just avoid the conversation. Also, like I could just go ahead and invite over the Squad. Sure.

"Friendship is really important, Niki, and you have to— Danny's up! Woot! Come on, Danny, come on, slugger!"

Phew. My brother trudged toward home plate. His pants were a little crooked and one of his socks was drooping to his sneaker. He stood beside the plate with his bat on his shoulder.

The ball went past him. I clapped. Yay, Danny, thanks for distracting Mom.

"Ball one!" the mom behind the plate called.

"Good eye, good eye!" Mom yelled at Danny from the bleacher. "Oh, hey, Terry," she said to the mom next to Marya. "Let me know when you have a chance about Danny's party, yeah?"

"Oh, yeah," Terry said. "I'm so bad at responding!"

"No worries," Mom said. "Whenever you get a chance!"

"I just have to—the weekends are so packed now that Tommy is on travel soccer."

"I know it!" Mom answered cheerfully. "We're all so over-booked! Oh, Marya—you'll let me know about Margot?"

Marya nodded. "So hard to pin these kids down, even the fourth graders, never mind the eighth! Can you imagine, when we were kids, the moms weren't at all involv—"

"Oh, so true," Mom agreed.

As the moms laughed about kids-these-days, I glanced at Isabel and Madeleine. They were walking toward us.

"Strike one!" the ump yelled.

Closer. I couldn't tell if they were looking at me, as their heads bent close to each other's, as they walked the path up from the beach. Whispering? What did I do so wrong today? Or, maybe: Were they inviting both me and Ava into their Squad? Could that be it? BE FRIENDLY, NIKI.

"Ball two!"

Raising my book to hide my face, I glanced in the other direction. Britney, on her green bike. And next to her, Ava.

On a bike. Her shiny black-and-silver bike. Her mom bought it for her in June. Ava had rolled her eyes and never rode it. She doesn't like bikes. She looked good on it.

"Ball three!"

My brother hadn't budged.

What if I slip between the slats and hide under the bleachers? Possible? Too late? Could I hide down there? Would anyone notice? What if I get caught between? And have to hang there like a speared bluefish, dangling, while the workers disassemble the entire bleacher system to free me? That would be subtle. Probably nobody would notice that.

"Ball four!" the mom-ump yelled.

"Good eye, good eye, slugger!" my mother yelled. "Take the base, you earned it!"

Danny dropped the bat and plodded toward first base.

"Maybe yell some encouragement," Mom suggested to me.

"I'm losing my voice," I whispered.

The four girls stood together, with their bikes resting against their hips, out beyond the outfield. They were too far away for me to tell where they were looking, and if it was mean.

The next kid up swung and connected, hit the ball in a dribbly line right toward the pitcher's feet. She bent down, picked up the ball, pivoted, and threw to first (*out!*). The first-base kid tossed the ball right into the glove of the kid covering second, who touched the base and then waited for Danny to make his slow way toward her, so she could tag him on the belly, for good measure. "Out!" the other ump called. "Two outs!"

Without breaking his slow stride much, Danny turned and lumbered back toward the bench. His coach called to him to come off the field, over to the side, *Come here, Danny!* so the next kid could bat, the game could continue. But Danny is not that easy to distract once he's doing something. He took his own sweet time of it, wandering through the infield, while everybody waited. The other adults smiled patiently at Mom, whose smile was one click too intense. "Attaboy," she called to Danny as she shrugged at her friends. They laughed supportively, but I caught the eyebrow raise that Madeleine's mom, Marya, gave to her best friend, Terry, as they turned away from Mom.

I don't know if Mom saw.

Probably.

She grew up with those women. Wonder if Ms. Andry ever told them to stand with their best friend. If so, I bet Mom was never the one left out. Maybe Madeleine's mom and mine were in their version of the Squad together.

Ava was waving. At me? I waved back, just in case. Don't want to leave her hanging—she gets really prickly about that kind of thing. Plus, maybe it really was Ava *and me* the Squad wanted.

*Friends are important and you have to . . . something.* Is there something I don't do, in terms of friends? Am I a little, like, weird, like Danny? Danny really doesn't have any friends but this one also-weird kid, Boone.

Mom smiled at me. "Call them over," she encouraged. "You know Ava, sometimes she needs to feel wanted."

*It's true,* I thought. *Maybe I haven't been attentive enough to Ava lately. Maybe she feels like she needs more attention. I shouldn't read so much. I should be friendlier, more fun. Sportier. I have to really work on that. Friends are important.* I waved a bit more committedly.

Isabel started waving. I felt my breath release, breath I

hadn't realized I'd been holding in. I let my book close on my lap. I smiled bigger at them. Isabel is the friendliest kid in the whole grade. She really is friends with everybody, not all exclusive like Britney and, in her quieter way, Madeleine. Maybe because her family is so huge, Isabel just gets along with everybody. Her smile is so easy, so natural.

I smiled back at her.

*Sometimes you're such a goon*, Ava tells me all the time lately. *Spinning your dopey little stories* . . .

I need to be friendlier, more chill, less intense. Prioritize social stuff more. Grow up. When's the last time Ava and I had a sleepover and did our jumping-on-the-bed contest, being the Olympic gymnasts and the announcers at the same time? It was, like, July. I should invite her to sleep over this weekend. Have some fun together. Ava is the only one I like to have over. If Danny has a tantrum, Ava and I hide in my closet and pretend we're orphan stowaways on a train or something. Maybe I've been too nerdy lately, too head-down in schoolwork. She and I usually nerd out together getting school supplies and setting ourselves up for a good start to the school year, though this year, I was maybe more into it than she wanted to be. But we both love school supplies. I even got two of those pink erasers I love so I could give her one, and wrote her name on it in Sharpie. We are such school supply geeks!

But maybe, despite those faults, the Squad was open to bringing in me and Ava, expanding to five. The pairing-up thing was just a blip, a weird gym nothing. Everything's fine! Why am I so un-chill? I was making a big stew out of a pebble.

"Ava!" I yelled. "Dude!"

Her face turned in my direction, her waving arm still in the air.

Oh.

They were waving. Just not at me.

At two boys on their bikes, coming down the hill at them. Bradley and Chase.

Six of them now, in a group, all looking right at me.

Awesome.

Even the ocean and sky behind them blushed.

I slumped down again behind my book and picked at the flaking green paint of the hard bleacher beneath me. Hating my mother.

*Thanks for the bad-vice, Mom,* I didn't say.

She was tipping her cute face up to the setting sun, like she was just hanging out on a nice afternoon, nothing wrong with her two kids, all cool.

All the other parents were busily looking at their nails or into their bags.

"Out!" the home base umpire called. End of the inning and my brother still hadn't made it back to the bench. Margot handed him his mitt and he turned around, toward my friends, the outfield, the ocean. Turned and kept walking. He has never caught a ball either. When Uncle Todd was trying to engage with him over Labor Day about sports, he asked

Danny, *What position do you play on your Little League team, sport?*

*Left out,* Danny said.

I still don't know if that was a joke on purpose or not.

Kind of a family tradition, that position.

I watched the group I was very much not a part of head back down the hill away from the game.

Usually that's not me, left out. Maybe it's just a weird day.

*Don't overreact, Niki,* I told myself. *Ava hates drama that's not her own.*

# 5

"I GOT THE game ball," Danny told Dad, taking the bowl of peas from him.

"Hey," Dad said. "Great job, champ! Did you get a hit?"

"Yeah!"

"A foul," I muttered.

"Niki," Mom said.

"I swung, and connected!" He took a spoonful of peas. Five of the peas missed the plate and rolled onto the table. Two of them dove off the edge onto the floor.

There's a reason Fumble sits right under Danny at dinner.

"Danny, don't dump the . . ." Dad said, and then took a deep breath instead of continuing, when Mom shot him a sharp look. "Cool, though. You swung! Can't believe I missed it!"

"It would've been a home run if it was over to the left a few feet," Danny said.

"Maybe!" Mom said, her voice high soprano, but a tight

smile on her face as she plunked a piece of chicken onto Danny's plate.

Dad passed me the peas. I took a careful spoonful and then a second, ladling them over my rice. No chicken for me, and a quick wish that Dad would please not make a thing of it tonight.

Extra peas!

*See, eating plenty, and peas have protein. I don't have to eat a dead bird to get protein.*

"Don't comment on other people's food choices" is an Ames family rule.

"I was the MVP," Danny announced, with his mouth full.

"Chew," Dad said.

"I'm chewing!" Danny yelled. A hunk of chicken dropped out of his mouth onto the table.

*Ewwww grossssss ewwwww.* I closed my eyes.

Dad breathed deep again.

I drank some water and when I opened my eyes, I kept them on my plate. Counted peas.

Isn't that a band?

Mom turned to me. I could feel it. "Niki?"

"What?"

"How's everything with you?"

"Fine," I said.

"How was school?" Dad asked. "Learn anything interesting?"

"No," I said. "Of course not."

"Niki!" Mom said.

I looked up at her. Her eyes were wide. Shocked? Angry?

"What?" I asked.

"I don't like your tone of voice," she said.

I didn't like her tone of voice either, but was I making a thing of it?

"Sorry," I said, and went back to counting peas: 27, 28, 29, 30.

"Can we please have a pleasant dinner conversation?" Mom asked, and turned to Dad. "How was your day, Jake?"

"Good," Dad said. "How about yours?"

"Busy, thanks," Mom answered. "Showed that house on Pinebrook. Mostly just gawkers. And the owners refuse to repaint or stage it. Nobody will bite, mark my words, unless I get through to them that they have to at least get rid of all their tiny bug-eyed dog sculptures, and take down their horrible curtains."

"I have work I have to get done after dinner," Dad said.

Mom's lower teeth were out in front of the uppers and she was breathing through her nose. She hates when Dad doesn't even respond to what she just said.

He helped himself to more rice, oblivious.

I let the rice and peas just hang out there in my mouth, trying to keep breathing through my nose so I wouldn't suffocate.

"Have some chicken," Dad said.

"No, thanks," I answered.

Mom was doing her breathing. The tension was so electric, I had to think fast.

"An interesting, well, it was weird—in gym today?" I started. The whole family looked at me, so, no turning back. "Ms. Andry said, 'Everybody stand next to your best friend.'" I imitated her as best I could. I'm not as good as Ava at that.

They all just kept looking at me, my whole family, waiting for the rest of the story.

"Isn't that—like, we're not even supposed to; it was just really awkward, everybody splitting up like animals."

"Animals?" Mom asked.

"In the, in Noah's . . . never mind."

"That does sound like a weird thing for her to say," Mom agreed. "She was always a mean old lady. But she said to stand with your best friend?"

"Maybe that's not what she said," Dad said. "That doesn't sound like something a teacher . . ."

"I know!" I said. "But that is what she said! I was there."

"Oof, that is awkward," Mom said. "So everybody has to . . ."

"Right?"

"It's so unfair to put you all in that position. So inappropriate."

"Exactly," I said, relieved, fortified. "We're not even supposed to admit we *have* best friends. And there we are, splitting like atoms . . ."

Dad laughed but Danny pointed at me with his fork and said, "The opposite of atoms, actually. Atoms split into two separate things. I think you mean like molecules."

"Okay," I said. "Whatever."

Danny yelled, "Atoms and molecules are not the same!"

"Niki," Mom said. "Please don't say *whatever* to your brother. It sounds dismissive."

"Fine," I said. "Sorry. May I be dismissed?"

"Niki!"

"Excused," I said. "I meant excused. May I be excused?"

I cleared my plate without waiting for an answer.

"Atoms and molecules couldn't be more different," Danny said.

"I'm gonna go do my homework," I said, at the sink, rinsing my rice and peas down the garbage disposal.

"Maybe we should play a game," Mom said. "Or watch a movie? As a family? Celebrate the *game ball winner?*"

"MVP," Danny said. "Which means Most Valuable Player. Because I—"

"I have some stuff I need to get done," I interrupted, imitating Dad.

"Me too," Dad said, not catching it.

"I have to watch my shows," Danny said. "I have four still unwatched. . . . I'm falling behind on two shows. You said I could, Mom. You did. You said. Remember?"

When I left the kitchen, I could hear Mom doing her deep breathing again.

# 6

I WOKE UP really early and didn't hit snooze even once.

I don't need to be a weird droopy emo kid at school. *Smiles, sunshine, and a quick cleanup make everything better!* I did twenty push-ups, twenty sit-ups, twenty jumping jacks, and twenty burpees—the workout Ava and I tried to do every day over the summer but sometimes I was lazy about—then got in the shower. Lots of conditioner. Shaved my legs while I let it sit in my hair, because my big out-of-control lion's mane of hair needs help to have any chance of being sleek and tame.

I'm pretty good at shaving my legs now. Mom warned when I begged to shave the summer before sixth grade that once you start, you can't stop. "You can't go backward," she said. I don't know why you can't. But I don't want to stop anyway. I like them smooth.

Smoothed my hair into a high ponytail.

*Just be positive*, I reminded myself. *Smooth. Nothing bothers me. That way, no matter what happens, I can't be hurt.*

A dab of the lip gloss Ava gave me the week before school started. Her mom bought one for each of us, just because Ava mentioned wanting it. Ava gets anything she wants, without even fully asking for it. She doesn't get an allowance or have any chores, she just . . .

No. This is probably why Ava is feeling annoyed with me—maybe she's right that I am low-key judgmental and critical. She doesn't always want to have to think about the moral thing, or privilege, she said one time this past summer. Maybe I am annoying. I don't want to be annoying. I dabbed on a little extra lip gloss.

My stomach was too clenched for breakfast. Ava and her mom never eat breakfast; they just drink a cup each of apple cider vinegar tea, grimacing the whole time. I looked in the cabinet. Pop-Tarts. No vinegar of any kind.

Mom was quizzing Danny on what he wanted to do about his birthday party. He was ignoring her.

"The Mad Scientist?" Mom suggested. "You like science. And wasn't that a fun party Niki had? When she turned nine? Do you remember that?"

"Yes," Danny agreed.

"So should I call her?"

"I don't want the Mad Scientist. I don't want a party."

"Well, we need to have a birthday party!" Mom said.

"Why?" Danny asked.

"Because, well, because it's your birthday! You already gave out the invitations, Danny, remember? I put everybody's names on the envelopes, you picked the truck invitations?"

No response.

"Remember?"

"You said no to the ones I wanted."

"Those were . . . We compromised, Danny. Now we're just talking about the theme, not the invitations."

"You said invitations."

"Let's discuss entertainment, buddy. Not about whether to have a party. You're turning nine!"

"I know that," Danny said.

"Can we get going?" I asked.

"It's still early," Mom told me. "Danny, do you have an opinion on theme? Or should I just make it a surprise?"

"I don't like surprises."

"Okay," Mom said. "What do you like?"

"Garbage."

Danny loves garbage. He loves the trash collectors and Oscar the Grouch and the garbage truck. It was cuter when he was four.

"That doesn't sound very festive," Mom explained.

No response.

"Maybe a firefighter theme?" Mom suggested.

Danny grunted. It wasn't a particularly negative grunt. His big, round eyes were steady-focused on the game he was playing.

Mom glanced at me, and shrugged.

I shrugged back. "Should we head out?"

Danny was slowly, slowly eating his cereal, still in his pajamas.

Some kids like Isabel are a team with their brothers and sisters against the parents, sharing secrets and covering for each other. Playdates at her house were always fun but so intense, just kids everywhere, everybody building something or making messes, so much louder and more crazytown than my house ever is. I always felt scared but also envious of the mess and joy at Isabel's, back when I used to go there.

Milo and Robby had a different kind of thing, not a hundred voices in their house but more like one, the two of them together. I remember when we were younger, when we still played together all the time, Milo told me one time that he and Robby lied to their parents and said Milo had tripped and fallen down the stairs to their cellar, when Robby had actually pushed him. I asked why he would lie to cover for Robby like that, when wasn't he actually mad? And shouldn't Robby get punished? Milo just shrugged. I think he had no idea what I meant at all. In fifth grade on school picture day when Milo was sick, Robby got back in line, messed up his hair a little, and said he was Milo, so Milo wouldn't miss out on having fifth-grade pictures.

They live next door to us. Those boys are always fighting with each other, but then they stand up for each other in a heartbeat. They're identical twins, and obviously they're best friends. They don't have to think for a split second if they're going to stand next to each other for a stupid gym class thing. If old bible Noah came around and said, *Load up the ark, two by two*, it's completely obvious Milo's partner would always be Robby.

It's not just because Danny is four grades behind me that I don't have anything like that with him. It's usually Mom and Dad and me, as a team, dealing with Danny.

Which is good. And also, not.

"I'll wait in the car," I said.

"Aren't you eating?" Mom asked.

"I'll take a bar," I said, grabbing one from the glass jar on the counter. "I can't be late today. I'm kind of lost."

"Okay," Mom said, flashing her broad smile vaguely in my direction. She obviously hadn't really heard me, or she'd be interrogating me: *Lost? What do you mean lost? Is everything okay, Niki?* Driving me nuts with her million questions. Instead she had already turned back to Danny. "Hey, Danny?" she was asking. "Can you look at me, so I know you're listening?"

*Can you look at me so I know you're listening?* I thought.

I put my sneakers on in the hall, grabbed my scooter, and went to the garage.

Mom drives us in the morning and I scoot home with Ava. Well, usually. Maybe I should start scooting to school. I checked my phone. No texts, nothing new on Insta or anywhere else. At least nobody was doing anything interesting, leaving me out.

Sometimes I wish we had a separate middle school here, like they do some places. Next year I'll be at the high school and not be late because of Danny, since I'll definitely have to go independently. I guess I'll have to ride my bike. It'll take too long to scoot.

Maybe I'm too old to be scooting already. I have a bike. I shouldn't be scared of riding it at this late point in my life.

# 7

AVA WAS WITH the Squad, sitting by their lockers, when I walked in. I put a smile on my face and pressed my shoulders back. I wasn't schlumping into school, some chubby, schlubby loser trying to disappear. Everything's fine. *Smiles, sunshine, blah blah blah . . .*

I waved casually at the Squad and kept walking.

"Hi, Niki!" Isabel called.

I glanced over. She was waving, smiling, no snark. She's the nicest of the Squad, super friendly to everybody, the one I like best by a lot. Much better than Britney, who was whispering into Ava's ear while clutching her sleeve and sliding her eyes sideways toward me. Ugh, Britney. Get over yourself.

I waved back, at Isabel. I could see being friends with Isabel, honestly.

"Oh, Niki!" Madeleine yelled. "Did you do the math?"

Being mean or normal? Friendly? Hard to tell with

Madeleine. *Are* they trying to get me *and* Ava into the Squad? Would I want to be? I mean, they *are* the most popular girls. And they're nice, really. Not nasty like "the popular group" in movies or TV. Fun, and happy. They laugh a lot. They whisper to each other. But there's nothing so bad about whispering. Maybe Britney is a little spoiled, but then so is Ava, and she's my best friend. Britney is fierce, though, where Ava is fragile. If you know her. Maybe she seems fierce too, from the outside, from a distance. Maybe even Britney is fine, and actually wants to be friends with me.

I realized I was just standing there in the hall thinking mean and hopeful thoughts about them instead of answering.

"Yeah," I finally said. "Um. How about you?" I balanced my folded scooter on my foot. Ava was bent over her crossed legs, not looking at me.

"I tried doing every problem," Madeleine said. "But . . ."

"You *tried*, but," Britney said, and laughed. Madeleine laughed along easily. Ava and Isabel joined in. I smiled, laughed a tiny bit, though I wasn't sure what was funny.

"In between texting Robby, you *tried, but*," Britney added.

Madeleine shrugged. "I suck at math; I can't help it," she said.

I smiled bigger, trying to look friendly. Smiles, sunshine. She was texting *Robby*?

*Are they a thing?* Madeleine and Robby? I mean, sure. Maybe. They're both very cute. Robby's less, like, sweet than Milo. Less thoughtful. She likes Robby better? I mean, if you could choose, why would you choose Robby? But, sure.

Robby and Madeleine? *Does Milo text any of them?*

"Niki's good at math," Isabel said. "Maybe she could help you."

"Sure," I said, too loud, too eager to stop thinking about Milo. "Happy to."

"You don't have to," Madeleine said. "If you're busy." She tucked her hair behind her right ear. It's her elf ear, because it has a little point on it. It made her super popular and a little scary in first grade, when she showed us all. She's always been tiny and delicate, so it made complete sense to me and Holly at the time that Madeleine might be part elf. And now, that Robby might like her. Some people like elves.

"It's fine!" I said. Too loud again. I meant to sound enthusiastic but might have overshot it and landed on psycho.

Ava turned and glared at me. Her heart-shaped mouth was in a bit of a frown. Did she want me to say sure, or sorry, no, not helping you, you elf, why don't you ask Robby for help if you're so busy texting him? *STOPPP.*

"I can look at it with you in homeroom, if you want," I said quickly. "Or not, whatever. I don't know if I got it all right, but . . ."

I did know. I got it all right. We were still reviewing the math we did last year. Plus, that's the thing about math—you can check. You know if you got it right, and if you didn't, you messed up somewhere and it's findable. Unlike in English essays or social studies, where you just write and write, and the teacher's opinion is unknowable. The super-fun humanities game of *Guess what's in the teacher's mind.* Though I have always found that if you throw in a few good vocab words like *inexorable* or *unfathomable*, you get an automatic A. They were all staring at me. My turn to talk again? Had they asked me something?

"Um," I said. "But, or, Ava could definitely help, I bet. . . ."

Nope, wrong answer. Ava shook her head and bent down over her lap again, doodling on her sneakers with her ball-point pen. Her mom doesn't mind that.

Ava and I like school. We like going all out on projects, especially. I mean, why not have fun with it? The Squad tends to do the bare minimum. Ava is really creative, super smart. She could probably help Madeleine, even with math, which is her least favorite subject, and she's sitting right there. But, no. Wrong. That, at least, was clear.

Ava is so confusing. But of course, that's part of why I love her.

I shrugged and went to my locker. It took some work to shove my scooter in. When I closed the door, Ava was there.

"Whoa!" I said, startled.

"Are you mad at me?" she whispered.

"No," I whispered back. "Are you mad at me?"

"No. You don't have to make everything about you."

"I'm not," I said. "I just, Ava, why are you being . . ."

"I'm allowed to have other friends, Niki."

"Of course you are," I said. "I didn't . . ."

"So just chill. Okay? You don't have to be all . . ."

"I'm totally, I'm chill! She asked me to help. I said okay.

I didn't, I, everything is great, with me. I'm not all ANY-THING. I'm completely chill!"

"Niki, don't lie to me, okay?" Ava's voice was excessively calm. "You're the most honest person I know. Don't start fake-smiling at me like I'm new."

"Did I do something wrong?" I was trying not to cry, hating myself for asking the exact question I swore to myself I wouldn't ask her today.

"No."

"So then, what's going on?"

"You don't have to make a whole drama of everything. . . ."

"I'm fully not, Ava," I said. "I'm just asking what's up."

"Let's just, let's not do this here, okay? Talk after school, maybe?"

"So, something *is* wrong?"

"Talk later," she said. "I just, I don't . . . I can't do this here. Okay?"

"Okay," I said.

She turned and hurried off toward homeroom.

I sat down against my locker.

I was in no rush to get there. Anywhere.

"You going to homeroom?"

I looked up. Holly. Her dark hair was a fluffy blur around her face, and she had some cute little barrettes in it. She was chewing on her lower lip.

"Yeah," I said. "I'm just, I'll be there soon."

She nodded.

"See you there," I said, to encourage her to go, leave me alone.

She nodded again, but didn't budge.

"I'm just, ummm . . ."

"Do you want a Fisherman's Friend?"

"A . . . sorry, a what?" Was she literally out of a fairy-tale book, like we used to pretend together we were—mystic fairy princesses full of magical powers, or trusted friends of sea sprites who would come to the aid of the lost sailors we imagined we could see just beyond the horizon as we played on the sand at Town Beach?

"It's a kind of lozenge," Holly said.

"A . . . what?" I was stuck on the idea she was offering me a tiny magical companion.

She reached into her bag, which looked like a burlap sack on a long, woven ribbon she wore cross-body style, and pulled out a small white packet, out of which she fished a small brown dusty-looking oval. She held it out to me in her open palm.

"They're disgusting," she said.

I had to laugh. "Then why would I want it?"

"They're also powerful. Powerful *and* disgusting. Much like myself."

I laughed. She's so weird and funny, and doesn't hold in either part of herself.

"They're not a drug or anything," she added. "They're from the grocery store."

"Much like myself," I said.

She laughed. "Exactly. And, like you, they open your head up."

"Open your *head*?"

"Not like a craniectomy or anything."

"A craney . . . okay, that's good, then, I guess?"

She tilted her head and smiled for another flash of a second. "Your sinuses. And they taste super intense."

"Um, so, no thanks," I said. "Why would anyone . . ."

"Sometimes, while I'm sucking on one, I'm thinking, wow, if I can manage this, the rest of my day is cake."

I laughed. "Okay, then," I said, and took it. "I'm down for a cake day."

She dug one out for herself and popped it into her mouth. "Good luck," she said as she walked away.

# 8

IN ART CLASS, fourth period, the art teacher, Ms. Hirsch, said we're doing a pottery unit.

"As long as it's not papier-mâché," Ava said.

I laughed, encouragingly. Ava hates papier-mâché. It makes her feel like puking. She can't stand anything gooey on her hands at all. When we had to do papier-mâché last year, I basically did hers for her, after Ms. Hirsch commented, *Ava's papier-mâché is always very . . . delicate. Maybe a few more strips of newspaper, before you quit, Ava?*

A few other kids smiled at Ava today—everybody knows she hates papier-mâché—but nobody else laughed.

Ava glanced at me, then away.

I forced my posture to stay stiff, no slumping in my seat.

Ms. Hirsch kept talking, but I wasn't listening anymore.

I was watching Ava, who sits next to me at our high art table, bend away from me toward Britney. She whispered in Britney's ear. The two of them snickered.

Ms. Hirsch said something about going up and getting your sketch pad and choosing a pencil or charcoal. She clapped her skinny hands together three times, telling us to begin designing the bowl or vase we'd like to make.

I wandered up to the front of the room when everybody else did, and took my pad and a black barreled pencil.

"You like pencil better than charcoal?" Holly asked me.

"I like being able to erase," I said. "It's my main hobby."

"Interesting," Holly said, and went back to her seat at the table near the window. I never particularly paid attention to Holly before, not since, like, fourth grade at least. She's always just, sort of, there. Nothing against her. Like, I didn't think of her negatively—just didn't really think about her. One of the weird kids. One of the randoms.

She was sitting across from Robby and Milo, with Beth and Nadine. Nice girls, kind of alt. Good at art. Maybe Holly wasn't a loser loner in need of my friendship. Maybe she had her whole own life going on, and she was not a lone porcupine unwanted by anyone, but part of a tight group of three, strong enough, and willing, to rescue me.

I watched the three of them, Holly, Beth, and Nadine, easy in their own skin and with each other—not smirking but actually smiling, not sliding their eyes in judgy ways at each other, sharks on the hunt for something to mock. They have looked kind of, well, if I looked at them or thought about them, like, ordinary or uncool, uninteresting, to me. Pencil in hand, I looked again. Trying not to stare, but still, trying to really see them as they are. While pretending I was looking out the window just past them.

Holly has short dark hair and pale skin, those thick glasses, mostly wears flannel shirts and jeans and, like, a hundred rubber bands around her left wrist. Nadine is big, dark-skinned, and tall, with deep dimples and braids, and a laugh you can hear clear across the room. And Beth, the shortest kid in the grade, even shorter than Madeleine but not as elfin, has unfortunate uneven bangs, bright blue eyes, and a mouth full of braces.

They're not loud enough to have a group name or really be noticed that much. I used to play with all of them when we were little. They were sitting on their art stools, chattering away, oblivious as ducks. Do they not feel left out? Actually, I guess they're not left out. They're together; they're fine. Hmmm.

I got a blast of feeling that almost unbalanced me, made me grab on to the teacher's desk. It was like a movie playing in my head, a vision of an alternate life where I'm at that table, happily chatting away with Holly, Beth, and Nadine, not trying to be popular or cool, not being snarky, not laughing all extra when boys make a nothing comment, not constantly checking Ava's expression to make sure I didn't say something that bothered her.

But no. That was a dead end. You can't go backward once you've moved on.

Sometimes it feels like I'm walking through doors that

keep shutting and locking behind me. I closed my eyes against the pressure building up behind my cheekbones.

"Do you need something else?" the art teacher, Ms. Hirsch, asked me.

"I guess not," I said. *I need Ava.*

I looked over at Ava, writing something on Britney's notebook. No way I could go back and sit next to them. But that's my seat. What to do?

"You sure?" Ms. Hirsch asked me.

I didn't answer, since the last thing I am is sure, and the truth of me not having what I need had nothing to do with art supplies. I was so good at answering teachers' questions until this week.

I went to my seat and stared at a blank page, my pencil suspended above it.

"Just sketch anything that pops into your minds," Ms. Hirsch encouraged. "Today is just about brainstorming. What could your bowl or vase or container be? What could it look like? What will it hold? Will it be painted or raw, decorated with found materials from nature, or plain? Tall, squat, square, fluted? Let your imagination run free!"

My imagination, running free, had nothing in it about containers. Instead it was stuck on me being an abandoned elephant, standing in the rain as Ava and Britney walked onto a boat. Why did Holly have to plant that dumb image in my head?

When I looked over at Holly, she was still chatting with

the other kids at her table. Ms. Hirsch lets us chat while we draw, which is why even the non-artsy among us love her class. It's like a break in the day, so much nicer than gym, which it rotates with.

I watched Holly. Milo was showing her something on his pad, his dark eyes searching her face while she looked at it. I couldn't hear what she was saying, and her back was to me, but I could see her pointing at something he had drawn, and her head tilted to the side, and I watched his face relaxing as she told him something. Something she was seeing in what he'd drawn.

His eyebrows were arching up.

She turned his pad back to him. He nodded. His smile melted slowly, not to a frown but to a softness.

Milo and Robby look almost exactly alike. You have to know them pretty well to know that Milo is slightly softer-looking, where Robby is a little more sharp-edged. But both of them have gotten to be really cute this year, their smooth tan cheeks, their dark eyebrows. They were scrawny, brawling, blotchy kids the past few years but I don't know, something happened to them during seventh grade and they, like, well, Mom used to say they were going to be such handsome men when they grew up and I was like, Ewww. *Watch, they'll grow into themselves,* Mom said. Which, *what?* What does that even mean? But, now, today, looking at Milo—I guess I get it a little. He grew into *himself.* So his nose and teeth look just the right size for his face, which looks, well, like a thing you could spend some nice time looking at.

Bradley and Chase are still loud and brawly, falling out of their chairs and tamping down their unruly hair with baseball hats that they get yelled at for wearing in school. They spend a lot of time laughing and being generally loud, knocking each other down literally and figuratively. The Squad flirts with them, and with Milo and Robby now too. Ava and I notice them, of course; it's impossible not to. But, like, we're not boy crazy or anything. We actually care about stuff like doing the math homework and being goofballs together and saving the environment (theoretically; I mean, we bug our parents to recycle, we decided to be vegetarians, we hate polluters), and doing what teachers say.

Despite my blank pad.

I started just sketching, letting my pencil do what it wanted. When I looked down, I realized what I'd drawn wasn't a bowl of any kind anyone would ever imagine, even free-running. It was eyebrows. Just eyebrows. Eyebrows over dark eyes that didn't look like anyone's in particular. But the eyebrows were pretty good. Pretty accurate. Like I captured something. The eyebrows were raised in appreciation and surprise, at hearing words I didn't hear. At being seen, maybe.

I was kinda proud of the left eyebrow, especially.

Ava glanced over at my pad, then across the room.

I shut the pad. Too late.

Ava leaned toward Britney and whispered something to her. Britney glanced at me, then at Milo, then back at Ava. She covered her mouth and leaned close to Ava, whispering.

The bell rang.

I crumpled the sheet of paper with the eyebrows, without fully opening the pad. I didn't need anyone seeing, commenting, judging.

I threw it in the garbage on my way out.

# 9

HOLLY CAME OVER to me at my new lunch spot, hunched over my notebook doodling eyebrows in the back corner of the library. I slammed the notebook shut before she could see.

"Why didn't you want to go to lunch today?" Holly asked.

"I don't know. Just needed a break, I guess. How about you?"

"I get that," Holly said. "I volunteer in here most lunch periods. Wanna help me reshelve?"

I shrugged, then shoved my notebook into my backpack. Nobody needed to spy on it.

Holly handed me a stack of books. I stood up and followed her. She pointed at the shelf where she wanted me to reshelve the books. "How's Danny?" she asked. Her voice was quiet but clear.

"Danny? Good," I said. "Why?"

"I was just thinking about how we used to do shows

with him when he was a baby," Holly said. "What?"

"Nothing," I said, realizing I was smiling. "I just, I forgot about that."

"Remember when we were playing with Milo and Robby that day in your yard, and we taught Danny to blow us kisses?" she asked.

"Yeah," I said, and laughed. "He'd kiss the air and then smack himself so hard on the face, with his full palm, and cry."

"But he kept doing it anyway!" Holly laughed too, imitating him, smacking herself in the face with her palm. "We all took turns saying goodbye and running into Milo and Robby's yard so he'd blow us kisses!"

"What a nut," I said.

"He was the sweetest little kid," Holly said. "So, he's okay?"

"He's . . . you know. He's . . . Why?"

She shrugged. "I help out in the after-school clubhouse for the younger kids sometimes, and he just, he seems kind of solitary. Which I totally get. But, you know, I was wondering if that's, like, voluntary."

"Oh!" I said quickly. "Yeah, totally. He's an introvert, I think. He's fine. Thanks."

"Okay."

"He's, I don't know." *Family business stays in the family.* "He's a little, I don't know. He's fine."

"Does he talk much?"

"Sometimes," I said. "Like, sometimes he'll follow you

from room to room explaining some fact he learned, or every detail of his shows that he likes, and I mean *every* detail."

Holly nodded so kindly, without saying anything, it was like a magnet pulling my words out of my mouth.

"Other times he just grunts or sits there silently." I swallowed hard. I hadn't meant to tell her all that. She was still looking at me, nodding slightly. "He's turning nine next Saturday," I added.

"Wow," she said. "Nine?"

It's the eye contact, I realized. She was like this when we were little, too, now I remembered. Holly was staring into my eyes, not glancing around to see who else was there, what else was happening, at her own fingernails. She wasn't impatient or anticipating or, like, judging what I said. Just listening. Is that weird, someone just listening? It felt super weird.

"He's having a birthday party," I told her. "But he doesn't want one."

"So why is he having one?" Holly asked.

"My mom wants him to have one."

She waited. I think she was waiting. I don't really know.

"He doesn't really have any friends, as you noticed. Is the truth. So, maybe that's why he's uncomfortable."

"Sure."

"I shouldn't say he has no friends."

"Is it true?"

"He's friends with Boone Fischer. Sort of."

"Uh-huh."

"And probably other kids. I don't mean to make him sound pathetic."

"You aren't."

"My mom invited the whole class."

Holly nodded without moving her eyes from mine. Was she hypnotizing me? Or just easy to talk to?

"But other than Boone, his only friends are . . ."

I stopped. Mom and Dad say family business stays in the family. You don't gossip about family stuff.

Holly waited.

Ava knows who Danny loves, and she thinks it's funny. Maybe she thinks it's endearing. She rolls her eyes because, well, that's just Danny being Danny. That's what Ava says about him, and it reminds me to be patient with him. And also why Ava is the only one I ever invite over. She's already used to how it is at my house.

"My brother loves the guys in the garbage truck."

"He's friends with them?" Holly asked.

I turned to the shelf and started wedging the books in, hopefully in the right places. "Not really," I said. "Like, I don't think he knows their names, even. He just loves to watch them load the trash into the back and grind it up. And how they all wave at him and call him Big Dan the Man."

Holly smiled. "That's sweet."

"What if nobody comes to his party?" I blurted out.

Holly didn't answer. I immediately regretted saying anything. Did it sound like I was dissing him? Gossiping? Trying to be cooler than he is? And honestly, if I were having a party this weekend, it's not like anybody would come to that, either.

"I mean, I don't mean . . ." I forced myself to take a breath. "Sorry. I don't know why I'm babbling like an idiot. Anyway, that's how Danny is. He's fine."

"Maybe I could stop by and say hey to him sometime."

"Oh," I said. "Um . . ."

"Or not."

"It's not, sorry. I don't mean to be rude. I just, my mom doesn't love having people over."

"I thought you said she's having the whole fourth grade over?"

Caught. "Yeah," I said.

"I shouldn't have invited myself over," Holly said. "I didn't mean to . . ."

"No," I quickly said. "It's not that. It's not you. Honestly."

"Sure."

"No, I just, I don't . . . I'm not, like, an invite-people-over person."

The bell rang.

"Anybody?" Holly asked quietly.

I shrugged.

"You used to . . . I remember being at your house all the time, when we were little."

"I just, I don't . . ."

"I'm sure you and Ava will work things out," Holly said, staring right into my eyes. "You've been best friends a long time."

# 10

*AVA'S FRAGILE.*

I was almost home when I stopped and sat down on the crabgrassy side of the road next to my scooter to think for a few minutes.

Ava had been ignoring me basically since Monday at gym. I wasn't sure how much more of this I could take. The idea of going to school again tomorrow, walking around so obviously alone and dumped, sitting in my assigned seats next to a best friend who would barely look at me—I just didn't think I could possibly manage.

So I texted her: **hey, you around this afternoon? Want to hang out for a bit?**

I wrote her name with a stick in the dirt next to where I was sitting, then crossed it out and wrote my name. I scratched my name out with my fingernails, getting dirt deep under them.

I wrote Holly's name. Smudged it over.

*Frick and Frack*, I wrote. That's what Mom used to call me

and Holly when we were little and best friends. I don't know what that even means. It was fun, though. Sometimes one of us would say *Hi, Frick* and the other would say *Hi, Frack*. It didn't matter who was who.

I smudged that over too.

Checked my phone.

No texts.

I couldn't think of anything else to text Ava that would force her to answer. So instead I texted my mom: **Okay if I hang with friends for a while this afternoon?**

I leaned back and looked up at the sky while I waited for a response. Clear, blue, no clouds. Weird to contemplate how a hurricane is heading toward Florida at this exact moment when the weather here is crisp and fully untroubled, I was thinking, when my phone buzzed.

**Mom: of course! Have fun!**

I knew she would say that.

I let myself sit there for another minute, thinking about weather, and how hard it is to know what someone is going through when your feet are someplace else.

Then I got up and scooted to Ava's house. My scooter could practically get there on its own. The Squad had tennis team practice, so unless she was sitting and watching them practice, I was pretty sure Ava would be home, without them—and I was right.

Her mom, Samantha, let me in and told me to go on up to Ava's room. Her mom used to be in TV commercials and was once on a soap opera, all before she married Ava's dad and gave up her glam life to give Ava a good, normal life in Maine.

Sam always smiles and then raises one eyebrow when she says that, about a *good, normal life in Maine.* She still looks like she's a mom in a TV show. A comedy, where the kids are smart alecks and she is spunky, her hands on her narrow hips, in the midst of their chaos. I'm always a little startled by how pretty she is.

Ava hates that, how everybody reacts to how pretty her mom is. Though in my opinion Ava is just as pretty. I've learned not to mention any of that. There are a lot of topics it's better to steer clear of with Ava.

I thanked Samantha and took the stairs by twos, past the mezzanine level where the living room with its huge windows looked out to the deck and the ocean beyond it. Everything in there looks like a magazine photo. Their house is always perfect.

The fact that a quiet woman named Masha lives in their attic bedroom and cleans up constantly might have something to do with that, but still.

Mom likes ours to look perfect too, but it's a different kind of perfect. The throw pillows on the couch always have to be diagonal, points up. She's very particular about those throw pillows, keeping them nice. When people are coming over, Mom dashes around cleaning in a frenzy, shoving things into closets and drawers. *You don't leave your dirty laundry out for people to see,* she says. Even though it's not laundry; it's newspapers and toys and art supplies and, sure, I mean, what Mom calls my sock brioches, which are just my bunched-up socks when I take them off and forget them in the living room. Mom hates that, because what if people stop over? What if people see sock brioches? The horror!

I knocked on Ava's door.

"Yeah?"

I opened it. Ava was staring at her wall, her hands on her hips, looking like a miniature version of her mom.

She barely glanced at me, so I went into her room and stood next to her, also looking at the wall.

There were messy rectangles of white paint on her pale rose wall. Three rectangles in a row, then three more beneath them.

"I don't want a white that's too yellow, but I don't want it too bluish, either," Ava said, pretending to be super serious.

"Yeah," I said. "That would suck."

She sighed. I sighed too. One of the things I love about Ava is how completely she commits to anything she does. Another is that it always feels like we're in the middle of a private joke together.

"What do you think?" she asked me.

I shrugged slightly. "They all look like . . . white."

"Yeah." She scowled at the stripes, then lunged forward with the paintbrush in her hand and made a big slash. White. I tried to match it to one of the rectangles.

She stepped back to where I was and made a mock-serious face. Like a perfect imitation of Samantha, I realized. Ava is deadly good at imitations.

"Mmm," I said, standing next to her in the same mock-serious pose, as if we were two art critics, or two Samanthas. Tilting our heads, squinting, assessing. Staring at splotches of nearly identical white paint on her walls. "They're all white, but . . ."

"There are degrees of white." She is such a good mimic, she sounded exactly like her mother. Who last year painted their kitchen pale blue, on a whim. My mom would freak completely out if I ever banged a nail into my wall, or taped up a poster. I honestly can't picture how Mom would react if I painted slashes of white on my bedroom wall.

"The just-right degree of whiteness," Ava said. "It's . . . elusive."

"Exactly." I smiled. She's so savagely funny. This is why it's impossible for me to ever stay mad at her, or one of the reasons. She's more fun, in all her edgy, subtle ways, than anyone. "How *many* degrees of white are we looking for, is the real question?"

"Pure white," she said.

"Perfect whiteness," I joked back.

"Racist," she said.

She mockingly calls me a racist whenever I say anything about the color of anything. It always makes me a little stressed, because, I mean, racism. But she's just kidding. It's important to be able to take a joke.

"Maybe I am?" I said, mock horrified. "Am I racist? How awful. Yikes. All whites look basically the same to me." She didn't respond, so I added, "They all just look white to me, honestly."

Her bottom teeth jutted out in front of the top ones as she looked down, fists on her hips, paintbrush dripping off-white paint onto the tarp. Actually mad at me?

"'They all just look white to me,'" she imitated.

"They . . ." I looked at the paint stripes. "Sorry. They do! Do they look, does any one of these white blotches look better than any other?"

"Blotches?" she asked.

"Samples. Rectangles. Honestly! You were kidding, right? Am I color-blind or are they all basically white? Is all I am saying!"

"No," Ava said. "What you're saying is that I'm basic."

"I'm so not."

"I'm superficial, wanting to choose the best paint color. My family is superficial. As if you and your mom are so in-tellectual and cultured and above things like paint."

"I think I'm above paint?" I tried.

"That? Right there? That is exactly what I mean," she said. "Fine, don't help me then. What are you even doing here?"

I pointed to one of the white stripes, the one closest to the hue of the extra slash of white. "This one," I said.

"You sure?"

"Hundred percent," I said.

"The others are too yellow, right? And this one's too blue?"

"Yup," I agreed. My fingers were all prickly.

"That's what I was thinking, the one I keep coming back to."

"That's a good sign," I said. "That's the one."

She smiled. Thousand watts, dimples deep. "Hundred percent," she repeated.

"I think I'm better than paint?" I asked her.

"I think you're better than paint," she said. "I do, honestly. Want a snack?"

"Okay," I said.

She dropped the paintbrush into a can. "I have to pee. Wait on my bed. Why are your nails so dirty?"

I shrugged.

"Gross," she said. "Don't touch anything."

"I never do," I said.

I sat down on the edge with my hands clutched together while she went across her room to her bathroom and closed the door behind her. I looked around this room I knew almost as well as my own. Something was wrong, though. Not just the paint splotches. What?

Oh yikes: all her books were turned backward on the shelves so you could only see the pages, not the spines. How creepy. It felt as off and unfamiliar as the first time I visited her room.

Ava's family moved here the summer before we started third grade. My mom was the agent who sold them the house. It was the first oceanfront Mom ever sold.

Mom and Samantha hit it off right away, especially when Samantha found out my mom had a kid the same age as her daughter, Ava. My mom said we had to be neighborly, and go over to welcome them. She told me to put my other sandals on, the ones I normally only wore with a dress, even though I was just in shorts and a T-shirt.

It was a pretty day, and not that far, she said, so she decided even though I already had the back door of the car open that we should walk over. I closed the car door. Their house was around the corner and down the hill, where the big waterfront houses are, behind the rows of tall spruces. Ten-minute walk, fifteen if you dawdle like I always did at that point, and especially that day, going to meet some girl I didn't know.

They had two fancy cars out front: one huge, one tiny with no top. Both super clean, no dents or dirt, I remember noticing. Their front door was wide open, no screen or anything. "Come in, come in!" Samantha yelled happily from somewhere inside. "Step around the mess!"

When we got into the huge entry hall, Sam was up on the balcony above us, looking down and waving enthusiastically. Ava was behind her, silent, frowning.

It was hate at first sight.

Ava trotted down the stairs behind her mother, both of them barefoot. She was wearing a one-piece green-and-white shorts thing with spaghetti straps, and her long wavy strawberry-blonde hair hung loose around her freckled, pouty face. I had too-long bangs and a too-tight ponytail, both of which suddenly felt ugly and babyish, and my fancy sandals, overdressed for my baggy shorts and dingy T-shirt, wrong, blistering my pinky toes.

The moms went out to the patio to look at the ocean crashing down the slope from their long back lawn. I heard Mom sighing as the door closed behind them. Mom loves the sight and sound and smell of the ocean so much. Her high school boyfriend, Jerome, who died, had a waterfront house. Our house is the kind Mom calls "plenty of charm." Meaning: small, and kind of falling apart.

"Can you do cartwheels?" Ava had asked me. She hadn't even said hello.

"No," I said.

"Maybe I'll teach you," she said, and did a perfect cartwheel, right there in the entry hall, empty but for the boxes. Not even a rug.

On the sides of the boxes next to me, there was writing in neat purple Sharpie, the same warning on each box: AVA'S FRAGILE.

Not: The Stuff in This Box Is Fragile and Should Go to Ava's Room.

Not: AVA'S. FRAGILE.

AVA'S FRAGILE.

Like a warning.

Ava didn't seem fragile, but that's how I misunderstood the message.

Mom had said to be nice and find something to compliment if I wasn't sure what to say. I should try to make Ava feel comfortable, welcome.

I said, "Wow, you sure have a lot of boxes."

"I'm depressed about moving," she said, doing a roundoff.

"Okay," I said. I didn't know what *depressed* meant, then. We were seven.

"She's from Los Angeles," Mom said when I complained about her that night. "Be patient with her."

"Does *fragile* mean *from Los Angeles*?" I asked.

"Not no," Dad said. When the two of them finally stopped laughing, Mom explained that fragile meant delicate, easily breakable. They didn't ask why I wanted to know. I remember being fascinated that this new girl was delicate and easily breakable.

The second time I had to go over with my mom and play with her, Ava had a fluffy pink lace comforter on her bed. The walls were painted rose pink with shiny white trim at the floor and ceiling and around her big windows, full of curlicues in the woodwork. I glanced out to the ocean, past her pale pink curtains, but I was much more impressed by the thousand stuffed animals, all arranged perfectly on her huge bed. It was only three days after the first time I'd been there.

No boxes anywhere.

"Your room looks very pretty," I said, complimenting because I still didn't know what to say to this girl I didn't know, a girl who was fragile.

She shrugged. "You want to see my toys?" she asked.

"Sure," I said. "Are you still depressed?"

"What do you think?"

I didn't know what to think.

She walked over to her desk. I followed her. There was a vase with three perfect white tulips in it, and matching glass jars of various sizes, filled with different sets of markers, with pink and white ribbons in various patterns tied around their necks.

It looked beyond fancy, the most beautiful accessories ever.

My stuff was mostly puzzles and crusty Play-Doh.

"Don't touch those," Ava said.

"Okay." I held hands with myself behind my back.

"Or the horses." She pointed at a shelf full of plastic horses, carefully arranged. "I collect them. They're very expensive. And delicate."

"Fragile," I said, thinking, *Like you.*

"Yes," Ava said. "That's why you can't touch them. In case you're clumsy."

"Okay," I said. I was like, *Fine. I don't want to touch anything fragile anyway.*

"Do you collect anything?"

"Enemies," I said.

"Weird," she said.

I agreed, so I didn't answer. Enemies? I had blurted that out because I was trying not to say *sea glass*, which, though true, suddenly felt babyish and boring.

Mom had said I had to be nice because Ava had just moved here from California so she had no friends. Mom had said she was proud of me for being so welcoming to Ava the first time.

"We can play a board game," Ava suggested. "I don't really care about those."

We played Sorry! until finally Mom called my name and I said, "Do I have to?"

That was our secret code for *Please let's go now.*

But by the time school started the next month, Ava and I were best friends. She hadn't managed to teach me how to do a cartwheel (still hasn't), but she had told me secrets and we played games of being orphans on the frontier or explorers in the rain forest. She was glamorous and creative, fragile and exotic. I remember feeling lucky that I had that forbidden thing: a declared best friend. Feeling chosen, and special.

The way I have felt ever since. Until this week.

She came out of her bathroom with fresh lip gloss on, sort of a raspberry color, and tucked her hair behind her ear exactly the way Madeleine does it.

She looked at me. "So. What's up?"

"Why are all your books backward?"

"It's a design statement. It's calming, the monochrome. It's sophisticated."

*You monster,* I didn't say. *How could it be calming to not know which of your books is which?*

"Did you come over to critique my room, my style, or my personality?" she asked.

"None of them!" I said. "Ava."

"Fine," she said. "Let's get a snack and go down to the water. We can have herbal tea; it's good for your skin. We don't need my mom eavesdropping on us."

# 11.

WE LEFT OUR shoes on the grass and walked beside the dock on the sandy part of Ava's beach to the water, which was icy cold but clear enough to see the pebbles below the surface.

The mug of herbal tea was welcome warmth in my already cold hands. I get cold when I'm stressed.

"What's going on?" I tried.

"Not much, you?"

"I mean it," I said. "Ava. Talk to me."

"You're the best friend I've ever had, Niki."

"I'm the only best friend you've ever—"

"I'm serious. You barged in here asking me what's going on. I'm trying to tell you. But if you'd rather—"

"No, I'm sorry," I said. "Go ahead."

"No offense, but, I just feel like we've drifted."

I resisted making a joke about me and the piece of driftwood a few feet out from where we were standing, floating alone on the water. "Drifted?" I asked.

"We're just, we're in different places, you know? I know you must have been feeling it too, lately. Since even this summer."

"Not really," I said.

"You're . . . Niki. You still want to jump on the bed and pretend we're orphans on a train; I'm, like, I want to shoplift a nail polish and figure out how to do cat-eye eyeliner and flirt with boys."

"Oh," I said. I stepped down into the water. Numbing my toes. *She wants to steal nail polish???*

"Don't take it personally," Ava said, behind me. "I just think, when you get that *gotta go* feeling, you know the one I mean?"

"Like when you have to pee?"

"No. Niki. That feeling like, it's time for me to go, I've been here too long, I need to make a change, this isn't right for me anymore. You know that feeling?"

"I guess."

"I just think when you feel like *I gotta go*, you should go."

"Obey the gotta go," I said.

"Exactly."

"And that's how you feel about—about me? Like, get me out of here?"

"See, now you're crying and making me feel guilty."

"I'm not!"

"It's so manipulative, Niki. You always do this, to get your way. You make me feel like I'm a terrible person and you're so wholesome, you'd never shoplift. So you cry and I feel like the worst. . . ."

"I'm not crying," I said. "I'm just listening."

"Fine, whatever you say. As if I don't know you well enough to see you're trying not to cry and making sure I know it."

"Ava."

"I just, don't you think, if we're really best friends, a best friend would want what's best for her friend?"

"Totally. Even if what her best friend wants is basically to trade up to a more popular group."

"That's not what I'm saying, Niki. Why are you being mean?"

I turned away. I hadn't been about to cry, but now I was. I didn't know what to do with my face other than hide it from her.

Two lacy-winged bugs, bolted together, landed on the piece of driftwood. I tried not to be jealous.

Ava sighed. "Why are you making this so weird and hard for me? Can't you just . . ."

"I'm sorry," I said. "Tell me what you want me to do and I'll do it."

"Just, all I want you to do is understand, and not make it such a big deal."

"But I don't understand," I said. "You want me to wear eyeliner and flirt with boys?" I left out stealing. Sorry, no.

"No!" she said. "Of course not!"

I turned around to face her. "What then? We haven't played orphans on a train or bed-jumping Olympics in months! What do you want me to do? Or not do? You want me to steal nail polish?"

"No."

"I don't know why you're mad at me, Ava."

"I'm not. That's not—you can't change who you are," Ava said. "I would never ask you to do that. Only a bad friend would ask that. Why do you always try to make me feel like a bad friend lately?"

Her nails were polished green. How had I not noticed that before? I turned around again to look at the water. The two bugs had left the driftwood. I took another step deeper. The bottoms of my jeans were soaked.

"We can still be friends privately," Ava was saying.

"Privately."

"Like, of course if something's going on, we can text each other. I'm not, like, breaking up with you, or some weird . . . We're just in different places, Niki, and I have to—when I'm with you, I feel like I have to be, like, honest, and . . . deep all the time."

"You can be any way you want, Ava."

"Not with you," she said. "I have to be real, with you. When I'm hanging out with the Squad, I can just be goofy and relaxed, not, like, smart."

"But you are smart."

"I just need a break," Ava said. "I don't want to probe how I feel about my dad being older and having kids from his first marriage, and my values, how they're like my mom's or different, how I'm like her or not like her, what I think about God and history and how I want to make an impact on the world."

So it wasn't just that she wanted to hang with the more popular crowd. It was also that she specifically did NOT want to hang with me.

"I just . . ." She did that hair tuck thing again. "Sometimes I want to be shallow and talk about fashion, and paint colors, and eyebrows."

"You want to talk about eyebrows?"

"See?"

"Sorry, sorry," I said. "I'm happy to talk about eyebrows, if you want."

"Niki."

"So, eyebrows," I said, hating the desperation in my voice, trying to make it sound jokey, fun. "What is even the deal with eyebrows? Right? Just a random extra stripe of hair across your face, who invented *that*?"

Ava smiled sadly. "Niki. You're the best person I know. But you know I'm right. Maybe we just need a break from each other. Okay?"

"What does that even mean, a break?"

"Just, let's not hang out so much for a while, see how that, how we . . . independence. You know? I have to figure out who I am as a person, not just as Niki's best friend."

I didn't really have an answer to that. All my words seemed wrong. I just listened to the waves lapping up around me.

"Aren't your feet freezing off?"

I shrugged. "We'll ignore each other?"

"Not ignore," Ava said. "Niki, I said . . ."

"Right. Just, like, does it include hanging out after school? Or no hanging out but you can text whenever, or only text in an emergency?"

"Niki."

"I just want to know what are the parameters of—"

"OMG, Niki, the parameters?"

"I don't want to mess it all up with my immaturity and wholesomeness, which is apparently what I do."

"Niki," Ava said, gently. "When I'm with you, you're like, you're the one person in the world who always sees right through me. The only one who loves me despite knowing all my hideousness."

"You're saying that and it sounds like a compliment."

"It is!" she yelled. "It so is. I know you're the best friend I could ever have, and I don't deserve you, and . . . don't you get it?"

"No," I said. "Ava, I really don't."

"I need to not be the bad best friend for a minute."

"You're not!" *Had I ever said she was bad?* "I never said one thing about—"

"I need to be not judged. I need to not have to be honest, or creative, or wholesome every single minute. I just need to be not, not reliant on you, the way I am, I always am. I want to see how it feels, who I am, when I hang out with . . ."

"With the Squad."

"Yeah."

I poured my tea into the water. It warmed up the whole ocean.

Just kidding. The warmth didn't even reach my toes, right beneath it.

"Sure," I said. "Have fun."

"You wanted to know the truth, Niki. And I always want to be honest with you, especially with you."

"Thanks," I said.

"Fine, whatever. If you need a towel before you go, you know where they are. I gotta go."

"But, Ava!" I didn't have an argument, I just wanted her to stop. "Can't we . . ."

She kept walking up the hill and into her house.

After a few minutes I put my mug down on the patio table. I walked around front to get my scooter. I realized as I cut through the Japanese rock garden beside their hot tub that my sneakers were down on the grass, but I didn't feel like going back to get them. Let Ava look out her window and see them out there. If that's *so drama*? So be it.

I scooted home barefoot.

It was . . . not as painful as my insides felt.

# 12

AFTER DINNER I told Mom I had to ask her something. She loves that.

I know if I told her everything about what was going on with Ava, she'd be concerned but also proud. She knows Ava is fragile, that she's sometimes hard on me—but she's proud that I have high EQ, empathy, that I'm mature beyond my years. It's why she can count on me to help with Danny, too, when he's having a meltdown. She and Dad think I am "really gifted" in dealing with him. I know other kids my age don't have to help their brothers or sisters with homework or tell them how to not be annoying, but they also don't get as much trust and respect from their parents as I get. Maybe it's thanks to Danny that I am able to be patient and empathic to Ava. Maybe I'll be a psychologist when I grow up, or a senator. I'm good at listening to people and finding solutions.

But even though it was the only thing on my mind, I didn't

want to talk about the Ava situation with Mom. Instead I said, "Can we talk about eyebrows?"

"Yes," Mom said. "I was thinking we should."

"You were?" *Is everybody thinking about eyebrows except me?*

She brought me to her bathroom and took out her tweezers. *Just a little shaping*, she said, and yanked out, like, a thousand hairs that were trying their best to stay firmly anchored to my face, while I sat on the closed toilet and complained. She laughed and pressed a cool washcloth on my on-fire forehead when it got too intense, saying *It hurts to be beautiful* and *Almost done, almost done.*

"Do you hate me?" I asked her.

*PLUCK!*

"I love you, silly!" *PLUCK.* "Look how pretty!"

She showed me my face in the mirror when she was done. It just looked like me, but blotchier.

"So much better, right?" she asked.

"I'm thinking of maybe starting to wear mascara," I told her.

She smiled, a little misty-eyed.

"What?"

"My baby's growing up," she said.

*Not enough, apparently*, I thought but didn't say.

"I'll buy you some tomorrow," she said. "You should try the hypoallergenic stuff, in case you're sensitive."

"In case?" I said.

She laughed. "My sweet, sensitive girl."

"Okay," I said. "Thanks." Though my plan was to wear

it to school tomorrow. Or to get in a fight with her, where I could say, *I am thirteen, not nine! You have to stop treating me like such a baby! You have to let me grow up and wear mascara and discuss eyebrows!*

But it was all okay with her.

She plucked a stray hair from between her eyebrows, leaning close to the mirror, and said, "I haven't gotten a single response for Danny's birthday party, and Sunday's right around the corner. I'm so stressed."

"Maybe people are just bad at responding," I said.

"I hope that's it," she said. "Poor Danny. I want to make this fun for him, make him feel special."

I nodded.

"Maybe you should invite a couple of your friends to come, Niki, so it feels more like a party. You know? Your friends are so lively. And fun. They're like my friends when I was your age, always giggling. And they could help out! I could pay them, if you think, like, as party assistants. My friends and I once made such a . . ."

"No," I said quickly. I did not want to get into her social successes or my own social problems. "I think that might feel like showing off, to Danny, if my friends are at his party."

"You're right, you're right," Mom said. "Of course. You're so wise. So much wiser than I was at your age. Or still!"

I shrugged. "You just had you and Auntie Bay, who was as popular as you, so you didn't have to think about . . ."

"Oh, Auntie Bay was much more popular than I ever was."

"Whoever shows up for Danny's party, that'll be fine," I

assured her. "I don't think Danny cares how many people come."

Mom nodded. She loves throwing parties. "I got so many cute things for it," she said. "Maybe you'll look it all over, give me your opinion."

"I should get my homework done," I said, getting up. "So, in a bit, okay?"

"Sure! You're so responsible." She kissed my head.

As I left, Mom called after me, "Would you do me a favor, if you . . ."

"What?" I asked, though I knew.

"Just, if you have a chance—see how Danny is doing on his book report? It's so hard for him, and you're the only one who—"

"Sure," I said.

"You're the finest kind, Niki!"

"You're welcome," I answered.

I went to Danny's door. He was watching something on his computer. I watched him, sitting there all glassy-eyed, then slipped into my room instead of helping him. I just needed a few minutes first. Fumble followed me and jumped onto my bed when I sat down. I floofed his ears and asked him how he thought my eyebrows looked. He wagged his tail, which I took as his opinion that they were okay. He had as much to say about them as I did, after that, apparently.

I was reading on my bed when Mom passed my door. Guess I was too slow.

I could hear Mom's sweet voice, trying to talk Danny into

starting his homework. Joking, sweet-talking, bargaining:

*Read for ten minutes*

*Read it to me while I make you a snack in the kitchen*

*Hey, how about if you see if you can get a title and first sentence done before the timer buzzes? You always used to love racing the timer*

*You'll feel better if you get some done and then you can take a break and watch one of your shows*

*Why is this throw pillow in here, Danny, you know that belongs on the couch and I like to keep it nice*

I was trying not to listen but it was hard.

*No, Danny, I know you think you can work and watch at the same time but*

I scratched Fumble's head. He was on alert, facing my door. Me too.

*Try half a page, how would that be*

*Danny, are you listening, because I need*

*Please don't crumple that throw pillow, Danny, that's a nice*

Fumble cocked his head, listening intently. More intently than Danny, clearly.

"Really?" I whispered to Fumble. "You know exactly what's gonna happen."

Fumble bobbled his head.

"Fair point," I agreed. "There's that. The one question."

The one slight element of suspense: Will it end quietly, with Mom basically doing Danny's homework for him? Or in a tornado, with Danny screaming and throwing all his stuff?

Fumble and I looked into each other's eyes. "I should've gone in there to help him," I whispered.

Fumble whined his agreement.

"I know. I suck. Selfish," I whispered. "Okay. What's your bet? Fight or no fight?"

Fumble, as a dog-only speaker, didn't answer.

"I'll take the deluxe blowout fight," I said. "You take peace process. Bet?"

I held out my hand. Fumble put his paw in it and we shook.

We faced the door and waited, listening.

Mom was still in there, cajoling, softly. Danny was grunting but nothing had slammed into a wall yet. Fumble was looking all smug, but I was like, *Just wait.*

Because that's how this dance goes, Fumble and I both knew.

Stuff could still start flying; Danny could start yelling, *NO NO NO!*

That burst, when it comes, always sends Mom stomping out of Danny's room to go vent to Dad, who then charges into Danny's room and bellows at him: *YOU WILL NOT TREAT YOUR MOTHER LIKE THAT, DON'T YOU DARE! PICK THIS UP! I AM WARNING YOU, DANNY, YOU BETTER* . . . and around that point Mom goes flying past my door back into Danny's room to get Dad to *Stop, calm down, let's not blow this out of proportion, Jake* . . .

. . . and then Dad, confused and undermined, tromps out. Leaving then-sobbing Danny to be comforted by Mom.

We have that whole dance down *solid*. We could win with that dance on one of Danny's favorite competition shows.

My part is to sit on my bed and watch. I am the audience. Me and Fumble.

We waited.

Silence.

Silence.

Moment of *it could go either way and . . .*

No crash.

"Okay? Let's just try it, okay?" Mom said.

No response.

"You can put your head on the throw pillow," she said. "And then after, we'll put it back on the couch nicely where it belongs, okay? For now it can be a special listening pillow."

When Mom started reading Danny's book out loud to him, I shook Fumble's paw again. "You win," I whispered to him. "Phew."

At least everything was calm.

Clam.

In first grade, all the kids in Snug Island Primary School make posters with their personal mottos. I remember Holly invited me over to make our posters together. She and I both made ours say GOOD BETTER BEST, NEVER LET IT REST, which is a thing my mom always says and Holly thought was so cool, at the time. We drew huge trophies, then meticulously filled in the shape with glue and then added gold glitter on it. We did it in her cellar. They had a whole art corner down there, full of supplies. It took us hours. Her family is very into projects, and they don't mind messes.

When it was his turn to do the project, Danny drew a circle with black marker on grayish construction paper. Inside the circle, he put two dots for eyes, and a straight-across line for a mouth. No nose or ears or hair. Underneath the blank-looking face, Danny had written in his mixed-case writing, *bE CLaM*.

*Be clam?* Dad asked him.

*Calm!* Danny yelled. *That is how you spell* calm*! The* L *is silent!*

My parents and I all made eye contact and held down our smiles. I felt in on the grown-up job of protecting Danny from the truth. And on getting how cute it was, his misspelling, his intensity about it. I loved that feeling, being on the grown-up team.

*Be clam*, Dad sometimes whispers to Mom or me, when tensions flare.

Mom thought it was so awesome, she had the picture framed. It's in the family room, as if *BE CLAM* is our family motto. Or maybe our family aspiration.

Mine is probably somewhere, in the cellar or whatever. Chunks of the glitter fell off on the way to school, so it was honestly garbage even that day.

I picked up my phone. Ava always complains about her mom to me. When I complain about mine to her, she's always like, *Oh, Niki, your mom is so easy on you, you have no idea.* But I thought, *Ooo, I could tell her about my mom and how she's babying Danny, how mad it makes me feel.*

But Ava didn't want me to text her. If I did, maybe she'd say that my mom babies *me*, too, and that's why I'm too babyish for her now.

I decided to text Holly. Why not.

**Good better best**, I texted her.

Sent it.

She could ignore it if she wanted or if she thought it was weird/random.

No response.

Why do I ever text anybody?

Maybe Holly is busy with her actual friends, Nadine and Beth. Maybe they were all looking at that text from me at that moment, like, *What???* I took out my eraser, useless for deleting texts. Or myself.

A knock on my door made me jump.

"Come in," I said.

"How's it going?" Mom asked, in my doorway.

"Good," I said. "Homework."

She smiled without showing teeth, a sad smile.

"Sorry I didn't help him with his homework yet. I just had to—"

"It's okay," Mom said. "Everything good with you?"

"Yeah, sure," I said, rubbing my eraser with my thumb.

"Okay," she said. "Your feet are filthy, sweetheart. Maybe take a shower before bed?"

I nodded quickly, trying to come up with an excuse for why my feet got filthy, and where my sneakers were. But she didn't ask. She just sighed and left.

My phone buzzed. It was Holly. I opened it, more eager than I wanted to be.

**Never let it rest!**

I don't know why that felt like air in my lungs but wow did it.

I hearted it, then turned off my phone. I didn't want to spend the rest of the night actively not-texting Ava. Let this response be enough, I decided.

When I heard Mom talking downstairs with Dad, I tiptoed back into her bathroom and found an old mascara, which I slipped into my pocket before I went to check on my brother, and knuckle him through the rest of his homework as usual.

The stolen mascara felt dangerous and heavy against my thigh the whole time.

# 13

MY VISION HAS always been perfect.

I could be a fighter pilot.

First test I ever flat-out flunked: the vision test at school today.

We had to go during fifth period before we were allowed to eat lunch. Ava and Britney were behind me in line to get tested. They groaned when the nurse kept asking me to try again.

"I think there's an eyelash smooshed into my eye," I said.

"Both eyes?" the nurse asked.

I leaned closer to her. "I'm wearing mascara," I confided.

"It doesn't matter," she answered.

"I might have allergies," I whispered. "To mascara. It could be. My mom thought I might. It's my first day wearing it."

Ava was rolling her eyes up to the ceiling.

"I don't think that's the problem," the nurse whispered back.

"I should go," I begged her. "I'm fine; I can see everything. I can see around corners."

"We have to alert your parents," she said.

"Alert my parents?" I asked. "About the mascara?"

"Did they take you last year to get your eyes checked?"

"I don't think so," I said.

"Ayuh," she said. "I don't see a form here."

"Maybe they did, though," I tried. "I think they did, yeah."

She was unconvinced. I had to check that all their contact numbers on the form were still the same, while the Squad shifted from foot to foot behind me, waiting for slowpoke me to finish the heck up.

"Thanks," I said to the nurse, when she finally let me go, and then wished I could take it back. What was I thanking her for?

I clomped outside in my boots, which Mom hadn't asked me about when I put them on in the morning. Sometimes I wonder if my superpower is invisibility.

I stopped in front of the field, where some kids were playing catch with a football. Isabel, who was already there, having aced the test obviously, put her hands up. Milo threw her a perfect spiral. She caught it easily and tossed it back to Robby.

"You okay?" Holly said, suddenly beside me.

"There goes my career as a fighter pilot," I mumbled.

"That's your ambition?"

"Just kidding," I said.

"Don't worry about it," Holly said. "It probably was an eyelash."

"Right? Do you go to get your eyes checked every year?"

"That's not a thing," Holly said.

"Oh, good."

"Then again, yes, I do, but I got glasses in third grade, so . . ."

The football was coming toward my face, I saw at the last second. But only because I had turned to look at Holly, so I wasn't paying attention. It wasn't a vision issue. I put up my hands. All my fingers nearly shattered. At least my nose didn't. The football fell on my foot.

"Oof!" Robby called.

"Maybe you do need glasses," Ava said, passing me with Britney.

"You okay?" Milo asked, jogging over.

"Fine," I said. "Just, you know, uncoordinated and going blind."

"Oh, good," Milo said. "If that's all."

I picked up the ball and threw it back across the circle. It wobbled a bit and didn't quite reach anyone.

"Yeah, because other than that I am totally being recruited to play football for a bunch of colleges already," I said.

Milo laughed. "Aren't we all?" he said.

"Hundred percent," I said. "Total jocks."

"Hundred and ten," Milo said.

"Yeah," I agreed, without remembering quite what we were even talking about.

"Yeah," Holly said. "We'll all be on scholarship."

I glanced at the Squad. They were all laughing behind their hands. I lifted my hand to my face and laughed too. Britney rolled her eyes, as she always does. I think it was like *with* me, *against* Holly, but it's hard to say for sure.

Also, that possibility did not make me feel better. Worse, actually.

Milo was heading back toward Robby. I watched him walk, noticing the smoothness of it, how he seemed to glide instead of clunking down each step.

That's why I didn't notice the football coming right at me again.

Ava lifted her hands in the air in front of me. Her sweatshirt came up so a tiny band of skin showed between it and her jeans. The ball hit her palms like she had magnets in them.

After she threw a perfect spiral back, the bell rang.

"Wow," Isabel said. "Ava just saved your life! You almost got hit right in the face with that ball!"

"Yeah," I said. "Thank goodness for Ava, because I'm apparently going blind."

Isabel gave me a concerned look.

"Right?" I said. "I'm fully tragic."

I rolled my eyes like Britney, so Isabel would know I was kidding, but she wasn't looking at me anymore. Isabel is so effortlessly cool, and I'm so effortfully not.

Going down the hill, I was in step with the Squad: next to Isabel, with Madeleine on her other side, and on the other side next to Britney, with Ava beside her. It had just happened that way. I could feel my cheeks prickling at the realization of where I was. Right in the hot center of the Squad. What to do? Act like that was normal? Drop back?

Holly was lagging behind us. Should I keep walking with the Squad or lag behind too? I didn't want to screw it up by being overconfident, or under.

"Hey," horrible Chase Croft said, jogging past us all. "Slowpokes!"

"Shut *up*," Ava said to him, and bumped Britney with her shoulder.

Even though I am apparently visually impaired, I definitely saw that.

Ew, Chase Croft? He looks like a villain in a comic book, all bony-headed and tough, with his close-cropped red hair and big hands grabbing at everybody.

Ava leaned toward Britney to whisper something, and the four of them, the Squad plus Ava, all started laughing at the same instant. Then they sprinted down the hill, after horrible Chase, away from me.

So. I think my eyes are not my actual problem.

# 14

MOM SAID, "WELL, let's check it out to be sure."

The nurse had made her feel guilty that she never brought me last year.

"It was just an eyelash," I explained. "I smooshed an eyelash. And that's not even a thing, to go every year."

"Yeah, so I thought, but apparently, the school thinks I neglect my children."

"If only," I said, which made her smile with crinkly eyes at me.

Still, she made me go with her to town, before I even got a snack or anything.

She must've called the glasses shop during the day, because they were waiting impatiently for us when we got there and Mom was all *sorry, sorry* as we were hustled into the back room, past the glasses displays to the medical area. I guess I had dawdled too long at the end of school, just casually hanging out in case anybody else was also hanging out, waiting for the Squad to finish tennis team practice, and wanted me.

The eye doctor had a scratchy voice, quiet and serious. She flipped through a bunch of different blurry lenses while I looked through the heavy binocular things, and she asked which is clearer, *this?* or *this?*

*This*, or *this?*

It was kind of fun, choosing. Up to me, just my opinion, nobody else's.

When she was done using all her toys and machines, the eye doctor crossed her legs and nodded at me. "So," she said. "I think you'd benefit from glasses."

"Maybe I just have a smooshed eyelash." I tried one last time.

"Nope," she said.

I don't know why it was bothering me so much, the thought of glasses. I hadn't actually planned to be a fighter pilot. Not really. Or an astronaut.

Not in any organized way.

Okay, maybe an astronaut. A little.

Never told anyone because that is sort of a little-boy thing to want to be, maybe. Honestly, though, I think I'd be good at it. I like confined spaces, and math. Travel. Looking through windows. Floating.

But probably meteorologist would be better. And there isn't a perfect-vision requirement for becoming the weather reporter, I don't think.

On the other hand, maybe I'm not pretty enough to be

the weather reporter on the news. Mom thinks I'm pretty but she's MOM. My mom. Not critical like Samantha is to Ava. Maybe if she were, I'd be more pulled together and attractive. Breezy Khan on Channel 2 News is gorgeous, and subtly sarcastic when the anchors try to joke with her about the weather. Her voice is low and cool, and she always adds in details like what falling barometric pressure means, or interesting weather phrases, like "severe clear" or "sea smoke." She's my favorite.

She doesn't wear glasses.

I don't like the idea of something being wrong. Especially with *me*.

The ophthalmologist herself had really cool-looking black frames and a serious manner to go with them, though. Maybe I could be like her.

Maybe I'll be an ophthalmologist when I grow up. There are probably jobs that are harder to spell, but I don't know any.

"It'll give me a new look," I said to Mom as we faced the overwhelming wall of glasses, trying for a good attitude, trying not to cry. An effort to make her not worry about me so much.

"What?" she asked, putting away her phone.

"Everything okay at home?" I asked. "Is Danny . . ."

"What? No. It's Samantha, it's nothing, it's—what did you say about a look?"

"Glasses," I said. "A new look. If I have to have glasses, maybe that's a good thing."

"True!" she said. "You always have such a good attitude. And you're right! It's always fun to reinvent yourself, get a fresh start!"

I turned away.

Maybe she thinks I'm ugly, and need to hide behind glasses. That's why she agrees I need a fresh start. Am I ugly? Is that why Ava doesn't want to hang with me now? And why is Samantha calling Mom, worrying her? Did Ava tell her she isn't friends with me anymore, at least at school?

I decided not to think about whether Mom was embarrassed by me, or how I look. Or how *hard* she was trying. How *big* she was smiling, whenever she caught me looking at her, but not the second before she caught me. Then it was frowns all the way down.

"You look gorgeous in every frame," Mom said. "I don't know how we'll ever choose!"

"Ugh, Mom, stop," I said. *Overcompensating?*

Ava's mom, Samantha, never says Ava looks gorgeous, even though objectively Ava is one of the prettiest girls in the grade. She and Britney, really, are the top two. But Samantha always says stuff to Ava more like, *What's going on with your hair, Boo?* When her hair is, I mean, I would give a kidney to have her hair, smooth and shiny and strawberry blonde, instead of my frizzy mess of black.

When my mom compliments me in front of Ava, I can feel the anger radiating off Ava, like morning fog on the beach where you can barely see your own feet. Mom thinks it makes me feel good to get compliments like *always gorgeous* and it kind of does but also kind of makes me feel pathetic, like I'll never actually be gorgeous so this is the best she thinks I'll ever look.

People say everybody gets better-looking and cooler in high school, but what if for me, this is as good as I get? And Mom realizes it?

When Danny and I used to run races against each other, I'd win by a mile. Of course. I was older and faster. I gave him a big head start and then bigger and bigger, big enough so I'd logically have to run full out to beat him if he ran his fastest, his medium, at all. I never ran full out. I was always rooting for Danny to win, every single time. I have never rooted for myself to win a race in my entire life. Even, like, against Ava. I spend the whole time thinking, *If I win, the other person will feel bad*—so then I can't. When I raced Danny, Mom would always yell TIE! when he finally crossed the finish line, way after me. It made both of us feel terrible. Mom was softening the blow of losing for him; I got that. He was way younger, but that's why I gave him a big head start. It was never enough. As I ran I'd be yelling, GO, DANNY, RUN RUN RUN, COME ON, DANNY, YOU HAVE TO RUN!

I knew it was out of love that Mom said TIE! *He's a little fragile*, she explained to me the one time I complained. Of course I thought, *Wait, what, Danny is from Los Angeles?* But she didn't know that was my memory of *fragile*.

"He doesn't have to be fragile," I tried.

"You're strong, and you know you won, so why would it bother you if I call it a tie?"

I didn't want it to bother me, and felt terrible about myself that it did, a little. But not really because it deprived me of a victory in a race against my little brother. I actually didn't care about that at all. But I remember wanting to scream at her: *He can survive losing a running race when he was barely more than walking! He won't ever RUN if he gets credit for a tie without making the slightest effort! How is he ever going to get faster if you tell him he's winning already? THIS is why he's always chosen last for teams at recess and gym class!!!*

But I swallowed that yell down my little-kid throat. I knew it wasn't (completely) her fault, just for saying TIE!, that Danny was always chosen last. Even if I wanted to blame her. Which would make it something she could easily fix.

Anyway, if I ever told her Danny got chosen last, she'd say that's a horrible, mean system and she'd call the school and make them change it, and everybody would know why, and who was to blame. Not that she'd be wrong. But still.

"Niki?"

I took the pair of frames Mom was holding out for me and tried them on.

Mom fake smiled and said she just had to text Dad to check in.

I wandered toward the sunglasses with the lensless frames still on.

As Mom frowned at her phone, it rang. She twitched, then answered and said, "Hey." So I knew it was Dad. I could hear Mom telling him that yes, in fact I did need glasses after all. She sounded a little sad about it.

I guess Dad had a lot of questions about the glasses situation because Mom was like, "Mm-hmm, I did. I'll tell you about it when we get . . . Mmm-hmmm, yes, I did. She's the one who . . . She is! Fine. See you soon."

She hung up and shoved the phone into her pocket.

I'm the one who WHAT???

"Everything okay?" I asked.

"Have we narrowed it down at all?" she asked instead of answering.

Her phone kept buzzing, but instead of answering it she just turned it off. She never does that.

"What's going on?"

"I just want to be here with you," she said. "Everything else can wait."

"Okay," I said, and tried not to grin like an idiot. I'm thirteen. I'm not sure I'm supposed to feel so happy about my mom wanting to focus on just me.

She held out another pair of frames she thought were cute. I looked in the mirror. I looked like a chubbier version of Holly.

Mom asked for my phone and took my picture in them. I made a pukey face.

"Gorgeous," Mom said. "But I can't tell if you like them or not!"

"I'm such an enigma," I said, sticking out my tongue.

"You so are." She smiled but like she was thinking about something else, then.

I put the Holly-like frames back. I didn't want to look like

I was trying to copy Holly, be two-of-a-kind with her. Better to be my one isolated elephant self.

Mom and I both tried on lots of different frames, including a super-blingy purple-and-rhinestones pair I almost had to get because they were so hilarious. The serious eye doctor shook her head at us but she was smiling, a little, then. We were *that* mom and kid, all relaxed and happy together, the perfect idealized version.

I imagined us from the outside.

We probably seemed so carefree and sweet. Just how Mom likes us to look.

Did they think we looked alike? At all?

She's so tight and toned, from running three miles every morning with Samantha. I'm vaguer, softer. And of course, no boobs on me, yet. Mom says she developed late so there's still hope, I guess. She didn't even get her period until she was almost fifteen, but she was an athlete. Like the Squad.

I'm not an athlete. I wish Mom had forced me to stick with organized sports, so maybe I would have that as a thing, like the girls in the Squad do. I don't really have a *thing*.

It's important to follow your passion, my English teacher last year, Ms. Kissel, told us. She was so loving and positive, even though she was also sarcastic and tough. I loved her. For a few weeks, I thought maybe my passion was my big pink eraser, but that didn't really lead anywhere. I still love it though. I like the color, I guess, and the shape, but mostly the possibility that no mistake is permanent. I can always erase it. Writing in pen stresses me out, which is why I got erasable pens this year, which is not strictly allowed, for tests, but otherwise my answers feel like tattoos. I always have my big pink eraser. But I don't know. Maybe an eraser is not much of a *passion*.

I sometimes study pictures of Mom to see if I look like her at all. We both have hazel eyes. Dad's and Danny's are bright blue.

If I have glasses hiding my hazel eyes, maybe I'll look even less like her. She wears contacts, not glasses, same as Dad. But no way I'm sticking my finger into my eye. I've seen them take out and put in contacts and it looks like they are poking out their whole eyeballs. No thanks.

After we made our final choice and got more eye measurements taken, we decided to have iced teas from the café next to the glasses store before we went home. On the sidewalk bench outside, taking sips from our sweating plastic cups, Mom and I stretched our legs in front of us, as if we were summer people here on vacation, nothing to do.

We were having fun, just sitting there in the slanted sun. Sometimes when it's just me and her, we get along so well. I didn't want to waste it.

"Maybe we should've chosen one of those crazier frames," Mom said.

"The purple," I agreed.

"Those were psychedelic," she said.

We both laughed.

"Psychedelic," I echoed, and we laughed some more.

"Those boots look so cute," Mom said. "You don't usually wear boots with those jeans. Is that the style now, with your friends?"

"I don't know."

She took another long sip of her iced tea.

She'd never say so, but I could tell she wanted to stretch out the time together too. Not just our legs. That made me feel proud, and then a little selfish, and then bad for her. Mostly I was just greedily happy for myself, hoarding the minutes and the calm, the sun and the joking.

When we got home, it turned out Danny and Dad had had a huge fight. So the rest of the night was about that.

Still, that time choosing glasses and sipping our iced teas all slow, that was special.

# 15

I TOOK A shower and used extra conditioner. The Squad all has silky hair.

Dried off, used a ton of zit cream, twisted my hair into a top bun. Considered push-ups and sit-ups but justified not doing them because I just showered, don't want to get sweaty. Looked up *what to wear to look cool in eighth grade.*

Answers included: don't try too hard, don't wear a long-sleeve shirt under a tank top (um, okay), maybe have parties with your friends to try stuff on so you can get their opinions. Great. Thanks. If I had a bunch of friends (and wanted them in my house), would I be googling this to get advice from random internet strangers?

Took out the black jeans Ava chose for me, the flowy top her mom bought me for my birthday, and a bra-tank for under (not over!) it. Cute socks, with cartoon avocados on them. Then, because I couldn't resist any longer, I texted Ava:

**Turns out I needed glasses!**

Send.

No response.

I turned off my light and tried to go to sleep, holding my phone in case anybody wanted to text me. But vowing to never again in my entire life text someone first.

I lasted maybe four minutes.

Texted Ava again: **oh and hey, could you bring my sneakers to school? I left them out back when I was at your house!**

Nothing.

Tried to convince myself maybe she hadn't seen my texts yet. Maybe she wasn't ignoring me, maybe the texts didn't go through. Maybe she didn't have her phone with her for the one time ever in her life.

Should I text Holly? Again? No. We're gym/yoga partners. That's all.

Text NOBODY. EVER.

It just felt like I should tell somebody I was getting glasses. Ava's not my only friend. Milo.

Milo? I should flirt with boys.

That's what they do, the Squad. What do they do, though? They just smile a lot, lower their eyes, laugh at any dumb thing the boys say. How do I do that if he hasn't said anything yet?

**Hey, I need glasses**, I texted to Milo and hit send before I could talk myself out of it. I stared at that for a solid minute, my heart pounding. Dread. How am I so bad at this? NEVER TEXT ANYBODY.

**This is Niki btw**, I added. Send.

OMG. Making it worse.

Delete delete delete. Why can't I delete a sent text? Why can't I have a time machine and just erase all my dorkiness? This is why my favorite thing is my pink eraser. Just erase everything please.

Can't go backward.

I used to imagine maybe someday I'd be world famous for wiping out cancer or warfare or pollution. Now my only ambition is to pull my most embarrassing texts back.

I sat up and retwisted my hair into a fresh loose bun on top of my head. Tried to find some music to listen to. Even Fumble had abandoned me. Every song felt like noise. I flopped back down and took my earbuds out. *Breathe*, I told myself. *Sink into the silence. Don't sneak into Danny's room to see if Milo and Robby's light is on.*

When I was little, it was so soothing to fall asleep listening to my parents' voices down in the kitchen, but now, I don't know. Not so much. They obviously thought we couldn't hear them. As if the wine they were drinking would dull my hearing instead of their ability to whisper.

Danny is the one who supposedly has excellent hearing. He tells everybody he scored the highest ever on his hearing test last year at the doctor's. Drives me nuts. *Stop bragging about your hearing; that is a weird thing to tell people about.* Still, maybe I have excellent hearing too. Maybe I could be a spy. Maybe that is my talent. A secret talent. Maybe a thing I should look into as a career? Way cooler than fighter pilot. Who wants to be an astronaut if you could be a spy?

Some spies probably wear glasses.

I tried to sense if Danny was asleep or awake. Using my spy skills, I concentrated hard.

Maybe.

I couldn't tell. Oh well. Maybe I'm not a gifted spy, either.

*Maybe I should go into Danny's room,* I considered. *Hang out with him. And if I happen to glance out his window . . .*

No. I needed to spy on my parents, not Danny. Definitely not Milo. What? Milo? Why was I even thinking about him? So much, recently. Weird.

"Danny?" Dad was asking.

I tried to focus in on their conversation.

Mom said that Ms. Chambers wants Mom and Dad to come in to discuss having Danny "tested." Ms. Chambers is the principal. She wants *what?*

"They just want to drug him up," Mom was hissing. "Any kid who's not completely compliant, they just want to get a diagnosis so they can tranquilize them into zombie-hood."

"We don't know that they want to medicate . . ." Dad started saying.

"Sure, Jake," Mom said. "I'm sure they just want to test him to see how brilliant he is. That must be it."

"Okay," Dad said. "That's not—"

"You know how they treat a kid with a diagnosis?" she demanded. "Especially a behavioral or psychological, or emotional? Emotional! Why do they have to make it a *disability*, like there's something wrong with—it's a, a stigma. A label. It'll follow him forever."

"But you said she suggested that there could be services he's entitled to?"

"That's the lure," Mom hissed. "That's the trick, so we sign the consent."

"So, let's not sign anything," Dad said. "Let's go, hear them out, and then we'll discuss—"

"I won't allow them to scapegoat my child."

"Suzi," Dad said.

"You're always so ready to blame him, to make it that he's purposefully, or that something's wrong with—"

"Suzi," Dad said again. "He threw a tantrum in school. We should be thankful he wasn't suspended."

"Thankful? Are you—thankful?"

"He terrified poor little Margot Hu and Ms. Broderick, so of course—"

"Terrified. What a crock of—he was frustrated!" Mom whisper-yelled. "She put him with Margot for a partner, and he said no!"

"He said more than—he screamed, 'I DON'T WANT YOU,' you said."

"Yeah," Mom said, with a slight chuckle. *"I don't want you."*

"Right! You don't think that's a little, I mean, *I don't want you*? What kind of thing is that to say to poor little Mar—"

"Did anyone pay attention to what he wanted?" Mom interrupted. "No! He's entitled to say no too! Doesn't he get to consent?"

"Suz, this isn't about con—"

"Yes, it is! He wasn't being heard! That's the only reason he threw his textbook at Broderick!"

*Yikes—Danny threw his book at his teacher???* I got out of bed and tiptoed toward my door to get closer. *And he yelled I DON'T WANT YOU at Madeleine Hu's sister??? Danny!*

"I know," Dad whispered. "I get that. I'm not blaming anyone. I'm just—"

"Well, I am."

"Me?" Dad asked her, his voice low. "Are you blaming me?"

"No! Why would you—don't make this about you, would you please, Jake? It's not . . . No, I'm saying, Samantha."

*Samantha???* I crawled to the threshold of my doorway.

"Samantha?" Dad asked. "What does she have to—"

"What she said about his birthday party, about maybe we shouldn't even—as if she doesn't throw the most over-the-top parties for Ava, with everybody invited. Do you remember when they rented that bouncy house? How over-the-top was—"

"Yes, of course. But why would that have anything to do with the school?"

"Well, you know she's tight with Ms. Chambers, or wants to be. She's always inviting her to our book club just to brag that the principal is there, and donating so all the kids can go on the trip or whatever, which she says she wants to keep secret. But does she? She told me, about paying the extra. Right? I'm her best friend, sure, but am I the only one she tells her secrets to? You know what I'm saying? Does she keep secrets? Or does she barter them? I'm just saying, maybe it's a coincidence, but——"

"He threw a——"

"I'm aware! But it's not the first time he . . . All I'm saying is, I should never have confided in her about the fact that I get frustrated with Danny. That's on me; I never should've admitted that. But she took what I confided about my child, about my most fragile feeling, and——"

"She's your best friend, Suzi, or one of them."

"Well, she's been really cagey lately about Danny, asking questions, and making these veiled, like, suggestions. And of course she was weird about Niki, too."

*ME?*

"You think Samantha complained to the principal about Danny?" Dad asked. I tried to telepathy to Dad: *Focus! Ask what Samantha said about ME!*

My phone buzzed. I dashed over to my bed to get it.

**Milo: Awww—that's cool, tho, no?**

"Not that she *complained*, Jake, come on," Mom was saying. "Could you give me one drop of credit please?"

"Suz . . ."

"When I asked her, yesterday and then again today, about what that thing was last weekend with the girls, remember I told you? The thing about Ava?"

*WHATTT???*

"I don't . . ."

"How she and those other girls acted when Niki—remember? I told you."

"Yeah, of course," Dad said. "Sort of? Remind me?"

"And you said I shouldn't say anything to Niki?"

"Definitely, I vaguely, yeah," Dad said. "I stand by that. You don't need to get all involved in her middle-school drama."

"That's what Samantha was saying," Mom growled. "She was like, *Oh, let's not talk about the kids; let's let them figure out their own mess.*"

*WHAT MESS???*

"That sounds, I mean, Suzi, you always say that too," Dad said in his soothing/warning voice. "We agreed. It's hard enough to—"

"I think Ava is excluding Niki," Mom whispered, but not quietly.

"Why would she do that?" Dad asked.

*Yeah, WHY?*

"I have no idea, but remember when I was at Samantha's last weekend after our long run? Ava and those other girls were there? Remember I told you how I said something about Niki, asked if they were meeting her? And they got all awkward? I told you."

"Yeah," Dad said. "I remember. Sort of."

Last weekend? What was I doing? Ava had said she wanted to stay in bed late.

I was just hanging around at home. I was here when Mom

got home from her run and she was all, How is everything going, Niki? And I thought, *Why is she so weird?* but she wasn't just being weird. She knew. She knew my entire life was about to blow up in my face. OMG OMG.

"They did, Jake. They got really fidgety when I mentioned Niki!"

"Okay."

*Ava was with the Squad LAST WEEKEND??? When she told me she was sleeping in?*

"Don't look at me like I'm crazy—they were in their pajamas, Jake. They had a sleepover and Niki wasn't invited."

"Shhhh," Dad said.

*OMG. OMGOMGOMG.* I stood up to get as near the edge of the upstairs landing as I could get without being seen from the kitchen. *Ava had the Squad sleep over and didn't invite me. I have just been booping around school, booping through my life, boop boop boop, without the slightest clue that my best friend had ALREADY DUMPED ME. Everybody must have known except me. OMG OMG.*

"I haven't told Niki, on *your* advice," Mom was whispering. "But now I'm thinking maybe I should because doesn't she have the right to know? If those girls are being little—if they hurt her, I swear I . . ."

"You what?" Dad asked. "It's girl politics in middle school. You said that yourself last weekend, and you were totally right. This is—"

"I swear I will never forgive her."

"Niki?" Dad asked.

*ME????*

"Samantha!" Mom said.

"For—I'm so confused," Dad said. "Is this about Niki or Danny—or you?"

"Family first. I will never—"

"Okay, before you . . . Maybe she—"

"Don't you defend her, Jake, don't you do it! I canNOT right now, don't even . . ."

"Okay," Dad said. "I'm not. I'm just saying, Niki is great, she's fine, and maybe we need to focus on what Ms. Chambers was saying about having Danny tested."

A crash. What was that?

Mom cursed.

"It's okay. I got it," Dad said. "Fumble, get away. Go up . . . Fumble! Where's Niki?"

I heard Fumble skittering up the stairs to my room. He jumped right into my lap, his tail wagging. I cuddled him and kept listening.

"My phone wouldn't stop ringing," Mom said.

"Don't, Suz. Step back. Don't pick up the glass with your bare . . ."

"The whole time I was showing the Tuckers' house to that crass, self-satisfied couple, who were like, *Is everything okay?* Fine, fine. Horrible. My phone kept ringing. Finally I had to answer; I thought one of the kids must've had a terrible accident. But no. There is *nothing* wrong with him! How dare they imply . . . He's challenging? Sure. He's also, thank you, smart, and sensitive, and they are a school!"

"Sure," Dad said.

"They have to teach each child according to . . . And then, to add insult, the nurse! She was like, 'When's the last time you took Niki to the eye doctor?' Seriously! It was basically bullying! They were ganging up on me. Like, *how many times do we have to call you per day, lady?* As if we just neglect our children! Is that what they think?"

"I'm sure they don't, love."

"She needed *glasses.*"

Was she crying? Because I need glasses???

"We both need glasses," Dad said. "So the odds . . ."

"That's not—"

"I know."

"Well, I'm going up to check on them," Mom said. "As always."

"Suzi," Dad said.

I let go of Fumble and dashed to my bed, faced the wall, slowed my breathing as I listened to her stomping up the steps. Fumble jumped up next to me, watched me. I could feel him wagging away, so excited with whatever this new game was.

I could feel my mother hovering in my doorway and then, one step to her right, at Danny's. No words. A few sniffs. She pulled our doors not closed but halfway.

Her footsteps, back down the stairs. *Step-squeak-step-squeak-step.*

I lay in bed, staring at the wall.

Fumble cuddled up next to me and we breathed in each other's faces.

Mom knew about Ava dumping me before I had any idea. She just let me walk blindly into traffic, into that most humiliating . . . She knew. She knows.

Plus: a meeting about Danny. Labeling him. Drugging him?

What do they actually think is wrong with him?

Does Danny have a right to know this is happening? Should I tell him?

We always say our family is so tight, so close and honest with one another.

If that's true, why were my parents whispering, or at least trying to?

And keeping secrets *about us, from us.*

My phone buzzed under my pillow.

**Milo: You okay?**

I couldn't even. I turned it off.

# 16

"WHY ARE YOUR parents at school?" Isabel asked me on the way from gym to lunch. I had been partners with Holly again. Trust falls are our major warm-up for yoga, which is basically all of us sticking our butts up in the air and waggling them around to make other people laugh. Whatever. At least it's not volleyball, my actual enemy.

"What?" I asked Isabel. I couldn't even make eye contact with her, knowing what I knew now.

"Your parents?" Isabel repeated. "I saw them walking in."

*Danny. The meeting. How was I supposed to explain?* "When?" I asked, stalling.

"I saw them walking in the main door, before fourth period," she said in her low, quiet voice. "I figured you were sick or something."

"Me?" I said. "I'm fine. I suck at yoga, but . . ."

She put her hand on my sleeve. "Good," she said. "I thought it might be about . . ."

"About what?" *Don't say Danny don't say Danny don't say . . .*

"Your eyes," Isabel whispered. "That you had to, that there was a problem?"

"Oh," I said, relieved. "I need glasses, turns out."

The boys were walking past us. Milo paused and asked, "Hey, Niki. You okay?"

"Great! Fine! Hahahahahaha!" I turned to laugh with Isabel, because flirting. That's what they all always do. Isabel looked alarmed.

"Oh," Milo said, slightly confused. "Okay." He jogged to catch up with his friends.

I weighed saying something about how cute he was to Isabel, or something snarky. Instead I didn't. Obviously, I suck at flirting even worse than yoga.

Isabel's eyebrows tented in worry. I weighed saying, *Your eyebrows are so expressive*, because eyebrows are an interest of mine! But again, NO.

"I know the nurse was concerned . . ." Isabel whispered. "And obviously Milo is too."

"Did you say, both of my parents?"

"Yeah," she said. "So, glasses . . ."

"Yeah," I said.

"I guess the doctors have to do tests?"

*She knows about Danny. Ugh.* "Tests?" (Stalling.)

"On your eyes."

"My . . . oh. Right," I said. "Yeah, they did tests. At the—my mom took me to the glasses place. You know, next to Scoops? I think your sister was working, actually, but I couldn't see . . ." *Don't look desperate, don't try too hard.* Isabel is so effortlessly friendly to everyone, it's easy to imagine she's your friend, but she is not.

"Sure, sure," Isabel said, nodding. "Because of your eyes."

"No, I mean because we were on the sidewalk," I said. "My glasses will be ready Monday, so, that'll be the end of . . ."

"Oh, so you just . . . that's all? That's a relief."

"A relief?"

"I thought I heard you saying something yesterday, about, that you were, possibly, going blind."

"I don't remem—oh! I was kidding."

"Oh!" Isabel visibly relaxed, almost wilted. It was so pretty how she did it. "I was so concerned, I just kept thinking of you all night last night, how you're tragically going blind, and how we'd all help you get around, and read the textbooks to you. We'd each take a night, and read you everything."

"Wow, Isabel," I said. "That's—thank you."

"I was thinking maybe you'd get a Seeing Eye dog."

"I think I just need, like, glasses."

"Okay," she said. "I mean, if it turns out something *is* wrong, we're all here."

"Thanks." *You're all at Ava's, you mean, having a sleepover I am not invited to.*

"So, it's probably just some random meeting. Don't worry, Niki. It probably isn't about your vision. Even though your parents are both here during the school day today."

"Yeah," I said. "Probably not."

"I have a cousin who's visually impaired," Isabel said. "She's amazing. You should meet her." Then she walked slowly, gracefully back over to Britney and Ava.

I decided to just read my book, on a swing, because when I looked over at Ava and Isabel and Britney, they all quickly turned away.

I guess Isabel was telling them about seeing my parents walking into school, or about me not going blind. The last thing I wanted to discuss was why my parents actually had a meeting today at school.

# 17

"MAYBE YOU COULD take Fumble for a walk," Mom suggested. "To the park."

"Or," I said, "I could let Fumble out in the backyard and I could stay in my pajamas, enjoying the morning."

"If nobody walks the dog, why do we even have him?" Dad asked. "Maybe we should take him to the shelter."

"Whoa," I said.

"Jake," Mom said. "That's not . . ."

"Your mother asked you to take the dog for a walk," Dad said to me in that quiet, angry voice that means *Don't even think about arguing.*

"I'm going, I'm going."

After I threw on some clothes, I dashed back downstairs and opened the hall closet where we keep Fumble's leash. He was practically doing backflips he was so excited.

Fumble isn't that big and our yard is fenced in. There is no reason he can't just go out there. He even has a doggie door so he can go whenever he needs to. But I will admit, he gets very excited when he sees that leash come out. Dad is right, I really should walk him more. We all should.

Speaking of which, Danny was in the family room, playing a video game. I noticed nobody was telling *him* to walk Fumble. Just me. One of the shows he watches like a religion drops Saturday mornings at eleven, so in half an hour. But he'd been playing that dumb video game for, like, an hour already.

"Bye!" I yelled when I got Fumble calmed down enough to hook the leash onto his collar.

"Have a good walk," Mom called back from the kitchen, where she and Dad were drinking their coffee.

Milo and Robby were out on their lawn playing catch with a football. Why did they have to look so cute? *Flirt with boys*, Ava had said. Well, here was my chance. If I could flirt with these boys I've known my whole life, maybe get one of them to like me, maybe ask one of them out, right now, Ava would see I'm not a loser.

"Hey, Niki!" Milo yelled to me, and waved. "What's up? Hey, Fumble!"

I ducked my head and went the other way, yanking Fumble to come with me instead of going toward those cute boys or the park like anyone normal would. The park is past their house, everything is past their house. But no, I walked up the dead end. What was even my plan? Great. No way I was walking back down, past them again, because what was I going to say? I got confused?

After I stood there for a panicked minute, I cut through the woods between the Bergers' house and the Leses', to get to the backyard of Ricky Landis, who is in the grade above me and once put mud on my head in kindergarten. I tiptoed quietly through his mother's flower garden to come out onto Rivage Lane, and loop the long way around to get to the park. Fumble kept glancing up at me like, *Really? This is our route?* But also wagging his tail, down for the adventure.

Maybe my goal shouldn't be astronaut or meteorologist but just to be as psyched about life and as confident in taking up space in it as Fumble, I decided.

When we got to the park, I threw a stick for Fumble to fetch a bunch of times. I should've brought a ball, I was thinking. I used to be good at throwing. So embarrassing, when I couldn't catch that football. Maybe I could work on throwing and be the first girl quarterback on the boys' football team in high school. Maybe I wouldn't have to flirt with them if I could be their teammate. Would that be embarrassing or cool? I don't trust my judgment on these things anymore. I used to know, I used to give Danny lessons in how not to carry his books (*stack them in size order, Danny; if you put little ones in the middle, it'll all topple!*), but now all my instincts are off. Like my eyebrows.

They'd probably do a newspaper article on me, if I were on the football team, though. I'd be famous. Maybe I'd even get to go on Channel 2 News and meet meteorologist Breezy Khan. I decided I would throw the stick at least fifty times for Fumble. Get some practice in. *I could be famous.*

The sky was that great September-in-Maine cloudless blue. It's the kind of sky pilots call "severe clear." I love that: severe clear. So clear it's almost harsh. Breezy Khan talked about that, in what to expect this weekend. Severe clear. Ahead of the monster storm Hurricane Oliana, which was currently destroying parts of Florida, and maybe making its way at us early next week. I love that idea. Not of Florida being destroyed. I'm not a monster. Of severe clear skies being pushed along in front of a gathering storm. "If the winds way high up in the atmosphere are too strong, they can shear apart a developing storm, keep it from turning into a hurricane," Breezy Khan said last night on the news. "You need calm winds to brew a hurricane."

"Maybe we really will get a hurricane, with these calm winds today," I said to Fumble, getting ready to throw the stick.

*Yeah yeah yeah*, Fumble agreed.

"We're in the cone of uncertainty," I told him. "Which is, to be fair, my permanent address."

I couldn't even be mad at Mom and Dad for basically kicking me out of the house to walk Fumble all the way to the park. I was feeling more revived than I had all week. Despite having made a fool of myself around Milo and Robby.

*Don't think about that*, I decided.

*What if they are still outside when we get back?* I wondered. What do I say about where I went, from up the dead end? I threw the stick for Fumble a few more times, contemplating never going home again, to avoid that terrible conversation. I could become a vagabond, is that what it's called? Or is that a kind of old-timey suitcase? Fumble didn't know either.

Fumble looked up at me, like, *Think of a better plan, Niki.*

"Maybe I should just wink at them if they ask what I did, and maybe say, *I'll never tell,*" I tried. "That is definitely flirty, right?"

I swear Fumble nodded.

"I'll never tell," I practiced on Fumble. He poked his nose at the stick like, *Sure, whatever. Throw.*

"I'm gonna be more like you, is what my goal actually is now," I told Fumble when he came back with the stick and dropped it at my feet. "Forget flirting. I'm just gonna be like, YES, life, that is AWESOME, everything, yeah, yeah, totally I agree. And if that makes me a baby, FINE."

Fumble's pink tongue flopping through all his black face fur was the only proof there was a dog there, instead of just fur and enthusiasm all the way down.

If I were like Fumble in girl form, everybody would probably like me.

I threw the stick again, a pathetic throw. My arm was heavy and tired. Maybe football won't be my thing. Maybe I'll just be super positive as my thing. I'm wholesome? Fine! Great! Yah yah yah.

"Wanna go home?" I asked Fumble.

He wagged his tail, totally psyched.

"Awesome," I told him. I decided, so what if Milo and

Robby are outside? I'll just say, *Hey, what's up?* right back to them. I don't have to flirt!

They weren't in their yard anymore, so I didn't have to try out my new personality on anybody right away. Fumble's tail was wagging so hard, it whapped my leg like a metronome while I sang to him, out loud, walking past Milo and Robby's.

We stumbled into our house, happy and delighted with ourselves and the world. I was about to yell hi, and that we were back, but something stopped me. Not sure what. Something about the tension in the house, or the pitch of Mom's voice, or, I don't know. Barometric pressure. The severe clear of my house.

I knelt down next to Fumble to unhook his leash, whispering *shhhh* to him.

They were in the family room, just around the corner. I closed the front door quietly and sat down against the wall in the front hall, with Fumble cuddled up in my lap, to eavesdrop on the rest of my family.

# 18

"... THAT IT'S TRULY nothing to worry about," Mom was saying. "So you really shouldn't take it as ... Danny?"

"Danny," Dad said. "Maybe if you would take off those sunglasses in the house, and look at us when we talk to you, it would ..."

"My eyes hurt from the light," Danny said. "I told you."

"Yes, you did," Dad said. "But—"

"Maybe the sunglasses are not the exact topic we need to be discussing right now, Jake," Mom said. "Danny, what I was trying to—"

"My show is on," Danny said.

"You're recording it," Dad said.

"Mom said I can't get more storage," Danny said. "Therefore, I need to watch—"

"Okay, but, Danny?" Mom interrupted. "Hey, buddy? Look at me please?"

Danny hates interruptions. He grunted loudly at her.

"Please just give me another five minutes," Mom asked. "Okay? We need to discuss . . . you need to . . . Danny?" Mom said again.

Danny grunted again. "I need to WATCH!"

"Do you understand what we're explaining about the testing, Danny?" Mom asked. "Because it's scheduled for next Thursday morning. But if that's too soon, for you, if you feel rushed? We can move it. There's no rush! It's not an emergency. It's not like, Oh no, something is terribly wrong! Hahahaha. Not that that would be funny. If something were wrong with somebody. I just mean, you might be a candidate to get extra services, and bonus time! And other bonus things!"

"I need more data storage," Danny said.

"We're not talking about storage now, Danny."

"I am," he said.

"Right, sure, but . . . Danny, I need you to, Danny, please listen for one more minute," she started again. "Look at me please."

Ugh, Mom, don't. Why can't she see he's not listening to her?

"Do you have any questions about the testing?" Dad asked.

"My show is on," Danny said.

"Or should we focus on your party tomorrow?" Mom asked. "Is there anything we haven't thought of, that we should do or take care of today? For your party? Danny?"

No response.

I knew what was happening even though I couldn't see any of them, or hear anything but the stupid theme music of Danny's stupid show: They were standing there staring at him. And he was happily watching his show, completely ignoring them.

Fumble looked up at me like, *What's gonna happen?*

I shrugged.

"Fine," Dad said. "Watch your stupid show."

"Jake." Mom hates the word *stupid*.

Nothing, no response from Dad. Or Danny.

The theme music from his show was blaring like a fire alarm in my head.

"If you have questions?" Mom tried. "Danny?"

Danny grunted, like, *Shut up.*

"Okay," Mom said. "Well, if you . . ."

She didn't bother finishing.

Footsteps, coming toward me.

I pretended I was still taking Fumble's leash off. Fumble got all excited, as if maybe we were going out for a walk again. I smiled at him, but his delight wasn't as contagious this time. Every bit of me felt heavy. My heart, my fingers, my eyelids.

"He needs to process it," Mom whispered to Dad. "I know that. I just don't want . . ."

"I know. So don't I," Dad whispered back. "Be clam."

When I glanced up, they were hugging. Mom's head was bent so her face, turned toward the kitchen, was hidden, her ear pressed against Dad's sweatshirt. His arms were wrapped around her and his head was resting on hers.

They looked like a statue, perfect and complete.

If I were a real sculptor instead of an eighth-grade maker of messes, I would sculpt them like that. I'd call the statue *Sadness*.

You could feel the ripples of grief coming off them all the way across the foyer.

They hadn't even seen me and Fumble there, left out and jittering in the entryway.

# 19

MOM NUDGED THE red paper tablecloth an inch to the left and then the same inch back to the right again. It was the third time she'd done that. It kept looking the same: like a red tablecloth over the picnic table on our back deck. But each time she adjusted it, she stood back and frowned at the tablecloth to see if her change made a difference.

There were five silver balloons that spelled out my brother's name in capital letters, bumping one another over the picnic table. Their strings were tied to weights covered in red crepe paper. Danny's favorite color is red, but the red balloons sometimes pop and balloons popping ruins everything for Danny so we don't get those anymore. The silver balloons don't pop as easily. You need to stick a knife into them, eventually. When they deflate so much they're just sad, hovering inches above the floor, it's time for them to go. They don't pop, even then. They just sigh like *whatever* when you eventually stab them to death. I remember from last year when Danny turned eight.

*Please let this year's party be better than that one was.*

I caught Mom checking her watch. She let out her breath and forced a smile at me. Not her normal smile like when a good song comes on the radio in the car, or Dad brings in flowers he cut from the garden. Her big fake smile that shows all her teeth, even the molars.

"You okay?" Dad asked her.

"It's three o'clock," she whispered.

"They'll come," Dad said. "Did they say they'd come?"

"Well, Julia said they had to be out of town for that wedding, so I know Andrew and Alicia won't be—"

"Right, but the other people?" Dad asked. "How many responses did we—"

"Danny handed out the invitations at school," Mom whispered. "To his whole class. I told you."

"I know. I just . . ."

"Don't start again about we should've emailed—I told you Danny wanted—"

"I didn't say anything," Dad whispered, turning away.

"He's in fourth grade. Nobody emails. . . ."

"I know."

"He wanted the invitations with the—"

"I didn't say *anything*," Dad growled.

I hate when they fight.

"I tried to call some of the—"

"Yup," Dad said.

Last year a few kids came to Danny's party, with their moms or dads. Madeleine came along with her sister Margot and helped me put out slices of pizza on the paper plates while the kids played the games my mom had set up. Danny hung back. I tried to act like no big deal, in front of Madeleine, and wished I had invited Ava to come so it wouldn't just be me with one girl from the Squad. Madeleine was perfectly nice, as always, but obviously we're not close. I knew she'd tell the rest of the Squad every detail of what a weird family I had. *This is why I don't let anybody come over,* I growled silently behind my fake smile. When the clown lady showed up, Danny started growling out loud, at Mom. The other kids all gathered around to watch the magic show, but Danny didn't like the clown so he had a major tantrum in front of everybody, and then stayed inside until the clown left, which was just before the cake.

"I don't like parties," he said to Mom, when she told him to *make a wish, sweetheart,* on his candles. After the guests left, she had a bad headache and had to lie down while Dad and I cleaned up.

This year Mom had gone to Party City and bought fire helmets for all the kids for the firefighter theme. There were three big tilting stacks of plastic fire helmets on the card table near the back door. I really don't know why she was doing this to herself, to us all, again.

"Maybe you should try on your fire helmet," Mom suggested to Danny. Not the first time she'd made this suggestion. It had been a long morning of setting up and trying to get Danny involved.

"It hurts my scalp," he said.

Mom checked her watch. "Maybe you could put it on just for a sec, so I can get a picture of you in it."

He moved his trucks around on the table, without looking up.

"Or maybe later," Mom said, like it was an exciting idea she just had.

"I doubt it," Danny answered.

I mustered a smile at Dad. He gestured for me to come up to the field with him.

"I'll show you the surprise I have planned," he whispered.

"Danny doesn't usually like surprises," I said, on our way up.

"I think he'll like this one," Dad said. "But I want to get your opinion on how to spring it, when the kids get here. You know Danny better than anybody else. So, tell me what you think."

When we got to the field up the hill from our yard, Dad pointed at the firepit.

"S'mores?" I guessed, already trying to figure out how to remind Dad that Danny hates them.

"No, doesn't Danny hate those?" Dad asked.

"Yeah," I said.

"No, it's: I'll make a fire in the firepit. Then I'll let Danny and the other kids hold the hose, maybe working together or taking turns, and put out the fire while they wear their fire helmets. What do you think? Fun, right?"

"Sure," I said. "Or, even if not all of them wear the helmets."

"Right," Dad said. He looked so unsure and hopeful, it

was like a flashback to what he must've looked like as a little kid.

"That'll be a really fun activity," I told him. "You could get a siren effect on your phone, if you want."

"Oh, good idea," Dad said. "Thanks, Niki!"

My father is very strong. Once, he was changing the tire of his car in our driveway and it came off the jack, and he just stood there holding the car up and cursing, yelling at me to get away, get to the grass. He looked like a superhero. But sometimes when it comes to Danny, he looks a bit like he might cry. Which makes me feel very sad and unsturdy.

The thing is, Danny really doesn't enjoy surprises much at all. I was thinking it might be a better plan to have a practice round of fire and putting out the fire, but it was too late because the party was supposed to be starting.

"Will you buy that siren thing for me?" Dad asked, holding out his phone.

"I can get it on my phone if you want," I said. "It's free."

"Perfect." He pocketed his phone as we went back down to see what was happening.

Nothing.

Just the four of us in our family still standing around our own backyard.

I set up my alarm to sound like a fire-truck siren but didn't choose a time, and made a wish toward the unlit candles on Danny's fire-truck cake that his friends would please start arriving. At least Danny's best friend, Boone. The guests were all already five minutes late and my mother's face was starting to look like a jack-o'-lantern on November fifth. Another thing that makes me feel unsturdy.

How can I be on Danny's side when he hurts my parents?

Danny was the only one of us who didn't look stressed. He was lining his new toy fire trucks up with the old ones. That's what he cares about. Not that his birthday party was supposed to have started and nobody was here yet.

Sometimes he seems like the only one of us who is okay.

But not usually.

After another few excruciating minutes, I put on a fire helmet. "Dude," I said to Danny. He didn't look up.

"Danny! Should we make sure there's enough candy in the piñata?"

"There is," Danny mumbled.

I didn't want to look at my parents, so I checked my phone again: 3:15. Nobody had shown up. I thought of texting Madeleine. Her sister Margot was supposed to be coming. I could find out if they're on their way, at least, make a joke about last year. What, though? Also, yeah, that's super normal for me to do, to text one of the most popular girls in my grade to find out why her little sister is blowing off my brother. Um, hard pass.

Ava. She said we could text each other in an emergency.

**me: So, this sucks: It's Danny's bday party and nobody has shown up. 15 minutes past start time. My mom is literally twitching. Advice?**

"Hey, Danny," Dad said. "Let's make a fire in the firepit!"

"Uh-uh," Danny said.

I couldn't look at any of them. No response from Ava. Oh no. She probably had another sleepover I wasn't invited to; they were probably all at Ava's in their pajamas looking at that sad, pathetic thing I had just texted her like an idiot, talking about my whole defective family. *Why can't I erase a text?* I rubbed my thumb against my pink eraser in my pocket. *Why can't I erase everything???*

I highlighted that dumb text to Ava. Nope, won't delete. Instead I copied it and sent it to Holly. Which I also immediately regretted. Was I looking for attention? Sympathy? Rejection? Just company? Why do I put myself at the center of the drama? No wonder Ava doesn't want to—

*Buzz.* I checked.

Holly.

"Niki," Mom was saying. "Maybe you and Danny could—maybe you don't need to be . . ."

"One sec," I said, and opened the text.

**Holly: That's awful! Is there anything I can do?**

**me: I wish—thanks, Holly. I just felt like complaining haha**

**Holly: Hang on, trash collectors, right?**

**me: ???**

**Holly: You said Danny loves?**

**me: Yahhh but???**

**Holly: They just came by—I had to run out with the recycling for my mom. Lemme see if I can catch them**

**me: Holly, I don't think . . . what will you do?**

No response. I looked up at Mom. She was sucking in on her lips, her trying-not-to-cry expression, and, yeah, the whites of her eyes had turned pink.

"Let's go," I said to Danny. "Let's make a huge bonfire with Daddy."

"Uh-uh," Danny said.

"It'll be fun!" I said. "We can throw anything you want to burn in there. Draw a picture of anyone you hate and we'll throw that in."

He glanced up at me. His sunglasses blocked his eyes and his mouth wasn't giving anything away. "Come on," I said. "I'll do it too. You don't have to tell me who it is, and I won't tell you."

"I don't hate anybody," Danny said.

"Really?" I asked. *How is that even possible? I hate most of my grade and, currently, all of your grade. Are you completely unaware what is happening right now, Danny?*

"That sounds fun, right, buddy?" Mom asked him. "Should I go get a pad and some markers? If you would rather write names, you don't have to draw faces. . . ."

"No," Danny said. "That's not nice."

"Or should we check the loot bags?" Mom asked, her voice a high soprano, an emergency.

"We did," Danny said.

"You know, I'm thinking, did I put four o'clock on the invitations? I know I was trying to decide which would be better, three or four, and now it occurs to me that maybe—"

"You put three," Danny said.

"I'll get kindling!" Dad yelled.

We all turned to him.

"For the fire!" he yelled. "Surprise! Fire! Put it out!"

"What?" Danny asked.

My phone buzzed.

**Holly: Bring Danny! Come to your front yard!**

**Now?** I texted back, but then I heard it. *Clank, clank, clank.* Danny's head swiveled around. Mom and Dad were oblivious.

"They already came," Danny said.

"I'm sure they'll come soon, sweetheart."

"Why are they here again?" Danny asked.

"Who?" Dad asked.

"Surprise!" I yelled. "Come to the front yard!"

*Please let this work. Please, please.*

Danny got up and ran, actually ran, around the side of the house. I followed him, not answering my parents' questions about what the heck was going on.

The garbage truck was parked right in front of our house. One guy, the biggest, was standing with his legs wide set on our front walk, while the driver waved over the top of the truck's cab. The short super-friendly guy with the beard was hanging off the back of the truck, yelling, "Big Dan the Man!"

Danny stopped on the walk.

I could see he was smiling even from the back of his head.

"We heard it was your birthday, Big Dan!" the bearded guy yelled.

"How old are you, Big Man?" the deep-voiced huge guy on our walk asked him.

"Nine," Danny told him.

"What? Nine! No wonder you look so strong. Show me a muscle, Big Man!"

"Which muscle?" Danny asked.

The huge guy made a bicep curl, his huge cantaloupe of an arm muscle bulging. Danny imitated him, and the huge guy reached out to feel Danny's skinny arm. "Whoa!" he exclaimed. "Check this bruiser out! Don't punch me, bro!" He held up his massive arms, pretending to be scared of Danny.

"I wouldn't," Danny said. "I never would."

"Good man!" the driver yelled. "So, you gonna help us grind this load?"

Danny turned to Mom and Dad, hopeful.

"Sure," Dad said.

"If you want," Mom said.

I wasn't looking at them. I was smiling at Holly, who was on her bike across the street. I did the *thank-you* sign. She made her hands in a heart shape over her heart and then rode away.

Danny spent the next half hour being shown everything on the truck, sitting in the driver's seat, working the tilt device and the scraper. I took pictures and videoed some of it so Danny could enjoy it again later. The workers refused to take the cash my dad offered them, after, but were happy to sing happy birthday to Danny and cheer when he blew out the candles, and to take loot bags along with their cake slices.

Danny's scrawny friend Boone got dropped off by his grandma at four, just as the garbage truck was pulling away. They both waved, and Danny recounted to Boone in excruciating detail what had happened with the garbage truck as they wandered to the backyard.

They decided not to smash the piñata, but to eat the candy out of the fire truck's middle as if it were a serving bowl, up in the field while Dad built them a fire.

Mom put her arm around me as we followed them up there. "How did you . . ."

"Shhhh," I said. "They just came because they're his friends."

"Thank you," she whispered.

"It was Holly," I whispered back.

"Holly?" Mom asked. "Holly Jones?"

"Yeah." I went to help Dad find kindling. I didn't want Mom's opinion on Holly right then. I know Mom has been proud that she thought I was in with the popular crowd. She likes Holly (she likes everybody), but she always smiled in a *we are the popular kids* way whenever I got invited to things with Ava and then the bigger crowd of popular kids, and was disappointed when I couldn't get myself to be interested in sports, couldn't hang with the Squad as much last year. She knew more about me being dumped by Ava and the Squad than I'd told her. I really didn't need to see the worry and pity in my mother's face over me being possibly dumped down to being friends with Holly. Not right then, thanks.

We ate cake while Dad made and then put out the fire, wearing one of the fire helmets. I videoed that, too. What a goon. At least Mom didn't have a headache this year.

After Boone finally went home, I stopped by Danny's room.

"Happy birthday," I said.

"Thanks," he said without lifting his eyes from his game.

"Did you have fun?"

"Best birthday ever," he said.

"You weren't—it didn't bother you that the other kids didn't show up?"

"I'm not friends with them anyway," Danny said. "They don't like me."

The reason people talk about heartbreak, I realized, is because you can literally feel your heart breaking apart. Right inside your chest, the cracking apart of it.

"Danny," I managed. "I'm sure they like you; they're just a bunch of pissant buttfaces."

He smiled a little, then said, "You don't get it."

"I do get it," I said. "Seriously. I think they suck."

"You don't get it because you're popular," he said.

"I'm not."

"Yes, you are," he said. "You're the most popular girl in your grade."

"I'm hundred percent not, Danny."

"You are," he said, matter-of-fact, calm. "So that's why you don't get it. The kids in my grade aren't pissant buttfaces. They just don't like me. I want to have more friends, but I don't. I'm sad sometimes about that. But even when I tell jokes or tell them interesting facts, I don't get more friends."

"Danny," I said. "That's awful."

"It's okay. I'm used to it. Boone sort of likes me, and I'm the only one who likes him. That's why he's my best friend in school. You're my best friend in the world."

"I am?"

"Yes!"

"Well, I'm kind of a buttface friend too."

He looked up at me, with his goofy sunglasses still on. "No, you're not, Niki. You're the finest kind, like Mom says. You made the garbage men come, you make up the best games, you're the most popular eighth grader, and you like me. Most of the time."

"Yeah, Danny," I said. "I do."

"Boone's my best friend in school, though."

"Okay."

"He smells a little like old clams."

"Oh no."

"Yes," Danny says. "He does."

"It was Holly who made the garbage men come. Holly Jones. Not me."

"That's what I meant. One of your friends. You're popular."

"I'm really not, Danny," I said. *Other kids confide in their sibs*. . . . "I actually am having trouble with friends lately, like Ava, the other day—"

"Yes, you are! YOU. ARE."

I could see the storm brewing. Not worth it. "Okay," I said. "Anyway, I'm glad you had a good birthday."

"My muscles are really strong," he said.

"Yeah."

"That guy was scared of me. But I would never beat him up."

"That's good, Danny. Use your power for good."

"I do," he said. "I will."

Dead serious.

I went back to my room and spent the rest of the night editing the videos and pictures I'd shot of his party for him. Not a great present but something, at least.

# 20

MONDAY AT SCHOOL I tried to avoid eye contact with Ava, or the Squad. In art class I asked Ms. Hirsch if I could move my seat to near the window. She asked if I needed more natural light. Okay, sure. I was happy she didn't realize I was just trying to get away from my ex–best friend.

Those three clunky syllables (Ex. Best. Friend.) in my head almost made me cry, right there in front of my clay.

Nadine and Beth were talking about the clay representing the patriarchy and they were all happily punching and pounding it, and then Holly was like, Yeah, the clay is everything that's keeping us down.

"Fight the clay," I said, and immediately wished I could suck it back in because maybe that's a stupid thing to say and who asked me and maybe they had a thing going, they weren't asking for my judgmental or weird or whatever input.

"Yeah," Holly said. "Fight the patriarchal clay into submission, and then we'll fill these bowls with something good."

"Yeah, clay, you stupid idiot," Beth said. And I don't know

why that completely cracked me up but it did. We were all giggling so much we were snorting, which was about the most hilarious thing and made us giggle that much more. Luckily, Ms. Hirsch is happy if kids are chatting or laughing as long as we're creating art. Which I guess we were, or at least we were sure pounding the heck out of our clay.

I glanced over at the Squad. They were frowning at us, whispering, rolling their eyes. I know Ava was thinking, *what a bunch of losers.* I ducked my head and smoothed my clay on the table for the rest of the period.

I was surprised when Holly showed up in the library at lunch. "You don't have to babysit me," I told her. "You can go hang out with Nadine and Beth. They're great."

"I know, aren't they?" Holly said. "I just like sorting books. It's therapy to me."

She took a stack of them off the cart next to where I was sitting.

"Danny looked happy," she whispered after a few minutes.

"He was," I said. "He was so happy, and I am such a jerk—I meant to thank you. I really did. I—that was amazing, what you—I should have invited you in, and I should have texted you after to thank you, and . . ."

"It's okay," Holly said.

"I'm the worst."

"You sure think about yourself a lot."

"What?" I asked.

"You were in the middle of thanking me for doing a nice

thing, but then you got distracted by yourself and suddenly you're the *worst*, which, obviously you're not *the worst*, so it turns into me having to tell you you're fine, or great, even. Why do you do that?"

"I don't know," I said. "I didn't realize I did that. Sorry."

"I'm glad it worked out. Danny looked really happy to see those guys. I didn't mean to criticize you. I was just—you apologize a lot."

"I do?"

"You can just say *thank you*, instead of *sorry*. I was happy I could help out." She turned and fit a book into its place on the shelf.

"Okay," I said. "Thank you, Holly."

I pretended to go back to reading but I wasn't, really.


After school, I shrugged into my backpack and was about to start scooting home when Dad pulled up and beeped. He lowered his window and called out, "Niki! Hey, Niki! Time to go get your glasses!"

I rushed to the car, threw my scooter into the back, and ducked into the front seat, low. "Hiya, sweetheart!" Dad bellowed.

I buckled my seat belt and sank down low. "I thought Mom was taking me. Later."

"She had a . . . Danny, Danny has a, had . . . Mom is meeting with Ms. Chambers. The principal. Right now she's there with Danny, and she might be hung up for a while, so, well, you're stuck with me!"

"I know who Ms. Chambers is."

"What?"

"Nothing."

"Okay." He started driving.

After a minute, as I was considering turning on the radio, Dad cleared his throat. "If you could launch yourself out into space," Dad said, "you'd see that the earth is a fragile blue marble spinning ceaselessly in the silent sky."

"Um," I said. "Sure."

"What I'm saying is, perspective."

"Okay, Dad."

"Things might feel like a big deal. Problems, at work or at school, or, like, with your body, or friends . . ."

My father and I, I realized, did not often have conversations all alone, just the two of us. Usually Mom or Danny would be there too, and they would be the topic, or the leaders of the direction at least.

"It makes everybody feel small and insignificant, catching sight of the earth from space," Dad said. "Have you been to the planetarium?"

"Yeah," I said. "The seventh-grade trip to the planetarium in Portland last spring?"

"I don't remember."

I shrugged.

"Did you feel that, when you went? Perspective?"

"I felt nauseated on the bus," I said. "Does that count?"

He smirked.

"For a couple of days afterward, I thought about maybe becoming an astronaut."

He nodded. He didn't say, *You'd be a great astronaut; you should follow that dream if you're really interested,* the way Mom would've, or *What a doofus,* the way Ava would've. Or, *I got the highest ever score on my hearing test* or some other unrelated news about himself, like Danny would've. He just drove on, so then I felt dumb for derailing his point about perspective.

"I know what you mean, though," I said. "About putting our own issues into perspective, by thinking about the universe."

He checked the rearview. "Well, that's good. Perspective is important. Keeps a person from getting bogged down in the small stuff."

"The thing is, though, Dad? The day of the planetarium trip, the one thing I was stressed about was if Ava was mad at me, because she was giving me the silent treatment."

"The silent vastness of space didn't make as huge an impression?"

"We don't live out in space. We live here."

"Yup."

"We're just, here. Stuck to our tiny patch of earth, sucked down by gravity and other people."

"Yes," he said. "I guess. But my point is, perspective."

"You're worried about Danny."

He took a long minute before he nodded.

"He'll be okay," I said.

He let out a deep breath, but didn't say any words.

"I mean, I think, I think it's a good thing, the testing," I said.

"You know about that?" he asked.

"Yeah."

"Mom said something? Or, did Danny talk to you about . . ."

"No," I said. *Whoops.* "He hasn't. I just, I think it's good. Maybe there's something that'll be helpful to him."

"It's not that simple," Dad said.

"I know."

"Your mom thinks anything they find could be a stigma against your brother, a thing he, we, all of us, have to then, you know, wear around our, like a sign on our foreheads, if anything is wrong with him, and . . ."

I searched for something to say to reassure him, but the truth is, it felt kind of good to actually talk about what was happening. A relief. I didn't want to make it go fakely away with a smile and a quick cleanup.

"And you're scared they'll find something wrong?" I asked.

He blinked twice, and then nodded. A tear dropped out of his eye.

"Yeah," I said. "Me too. Scared they'll find something. Scared they won't."

"Yeah," he said.

We just sat there in the car, staring out the front window.

"Sometimes knowing doesn't solve the problem," Dad

said quietly. "Sometimes there isn't a cure. And no amount of perspective that I can come up with makes it okay to know my kid is suffering, and there's nothing I . . ."

He closed his eyes but tears fell out of them anyway. He didn't wipe them away. He just let them fall onto his lap.

We sat there together for a few minutes.

I had never seen him cry before and I wasn't sure what a person should do when her father is sitting in the driver's seat in a car that's off and he's crying.

# 21

BREAKING NEWS: TREES have *individual leaves*.

I just want to spend the rest of my life looking at things. That's my big new ambition. The outlines of things, the separateness of each thing from every other thing in the whole universe. It wasn't even an insight (ahahahahaha insight because sight OUT into the world, everything is suddenly IN SIGHT) I could legit describe to my father, who was like, *Niki, are you okay?*

How do you answer without sounding like Looney Tunes when your entire thought is *WOW is THIS what everybody's been seeing all this time? All these sharp edges and OH MY GOD YOUR FACE IS SO SPECIFIC, you have individual eyelashes!*

"I'm fine," I said. "Thanks."

"Want some ice cream?"

"Ice cream," I echoed. I didn't even care, didn't know if I could handle any more sensory input than *holy crap there are specks of color in the sidewalk.*

Dad was a few steps in front of me. I was watching my shockingly *detailed* sneakers swing into my field of vision beneath me on the sidewalk, heading toward Scoops. Field of vision. Like it's a field, anywhere you look. Everything is a field, with individual blades of grass each waving around trying to attract your attention and let you know they aren't just a blur of generalized field but each is an individual, singular green pillar, unique in all the world, bold and extraordinary. *Hello, I am a particular blade of grass in your field of . . .*

"Niki?" Dad was asking.

I looked up. He has nubs of black hairs poking through his face skin where I thought he had a rub of shadow. *Does everybody see all these details all day long, and still function?*

*I am so impressed with everybody, how well they handle all this information coming at them all the time. I've had these magical glasses pressing heavily down on my nose for five minutes and might need to sleep for eleven hours straight from the intensity.*

Dad was holding open the door of Scoops, letting all their cold air out into the humid stillness. I walked in. "Thanks."

"Getting used to the glasses?" he asked.

"Um, no! Not yet."

"I remember being completely shocked by how chalk looked on the chalkboard in my third-grade classroom, the day I got mine," Dad said. "The texture. The unevenness."

"Oh man," I said. "I just, I want to look at everything."

He put his arm around me. It was warm and heavy, reassuringly solid.

I looked around the shop. We were the only two customers.

Behind the counter were two servers: Isabel's older sister Kallista, and a guy over six feet tall and broad, who was rocking slightly on his feet and humming to himself. His hair was standing up in clumps and his eyes were down. His humming was getting louder, and a few grunts slipped in.

"Hi," I said to Kallista.

"Niki!" she said. "Hi, Mr. Ames."

"Hi," my dad said.

"New glasses?" Kallista asked. She graduated from high school last spring, and Isabel said she's working here at Scoops and also tutoring for this whole year to make money for college. I don't think my parents will make me, or let me, do that. There are so many kids in their family, though; that's what they do. Kallista is eighteen, beautiful, super cool—and still friendly enough to notice new glasses on her little sister's semi-friend. I was so flattered that she remembered my name, I couldn't speak.

I nodded.

"They look awesome on you!"

I could feel my cheeks heating up. Kallista is so pretty, even prettier than Isabel.

"Do you know my cousin Rhys?" she was asking me.

"No," I managed. I didn't want to stare at Kallista and grin like an idiot. I didn't want Kallista to think I was rude, or a dork. I didn't want to stare at Rhys, either. I didn't want to make him feel uncomfortable, which he clearly was feeling anyway. But then that felt rude, and also I really wanted to look at everything. Including Kallista, including him. To notice everything. "Hi, Rhys," I managed.

Rhys made a grunting sound. Kallista smiled at him. He didn't even notice. What a waste of that smile.

"It's his first day working here," she told us. "Right, Rhysie?"

He rocked and waggled his hands around a bit. Maybe waving hello at us or maybe just dealing with the blue latex gloves on his big hands. He was holding them parallel to the floor, fingers splayed. Probably the latex felt weird on his skin, I was thinking. Maybe it felt to him like my new glasses felt to me: so much information coming in over the nerves, too much to sort through. I considered telling him that, that I knew just how he was feeling, but then that felt presumptuous. Maybe he wasn't feeling that at all, how would I know? And why would he or anyone care about how buzzy my head felt behind these new glasses?

"He's savage at scooping already," Kallista was saying. "Super-strong wrists! Just tell him what flavor you want, and we're on it."

"Okay," I said, instead of making a thing of myself or him. How does Kallista have such smooth skin? I looked down to study the flavor choices. Is that what people think Danny is like, like Rhys, if they think something is wrong with him? Is that what Danny will be like when he gets older? If so, will I be as positive toward him as Kallista is toward Rhys? I should be more positive toward Danny.

Also, wow, the chips in chocolate chip ice cream are curved little planks of chocolate.

"Coffee please," my dad was saying. "In a cup. Do you have coconut to put on top today?"

"We do!" Kallista said. "I'm on toppings today. Free jimmies if you want 'em."

"No, thanks," Dad said. "Just coconut."

Rhys scooped a huge amount of ice cream into a small cup and handed it to Kallista. "So generous," Dad said. "Thanks!"

Kallista rained some coconut flakes down on top. "My lucky day," Dad said.

I looked up at Rhys through my new glasses. He was chewing on his lower lip and rocking again. I really wanted to say something nice to him, to connect. I just didn't know what, and didn't want to embarrass him. Or myself.

Defeated, I mumbled, "Chocolate chip please, in a cone?"

He grabbed a cone with one hand and started scooping the chocolate chip with the other. But when he brought them together, the cone smashed, collapsing in on itself.

His mouth turned down. His two hands, one with the destroyed cone and the other with the metal scooper and ice cream starting to drip off it, were parallel, in front of his face, like boxing gloves at the start of a bout. His grunting got louder and he started shaking his head. "No," he said angrily. "No!"

"It's okay," I said. "Rhys, listen to me. It's okay!"

"Stupid!" Rhys grunted. "Stupid, stupid, stupid!"

"Rhys, you're not stupid," Kallista said, stepping closer to him. "You're doing a really good job."

"You are," I agreed. "You're not stupid, I swear."

"We don't talk to him like that, Niki," Kallista said to me, her face all blotchy red. "I don't know where he learned that. I swear."

"That's the way I like it best," I said, loud. "Rhys! That is exactly, THANK YOU. My favorite way! It's good. It's okay. You're good."

He chewed on his lip harder but he'd stopped yelling.

"Can you put the ice cream in a cup?" I asked him. "One of the medium cups?"

He banged the scooper, ice cream side up, onto the counter, and got a medium cup. Then he picked the scooper up and dumped the scoop of chocolate chip ice cream into it.

"And now, crumble the cone, right on top?" I asked. "Please?"

He hesitated. A small smile twitched his mouth. He moved his hand over to the melty bowl of ice cream and crushed the cone above it. There were some shards of cone but mostly it was cone-powder.

He handed it over the top of the glass enclosure to me.

I reached up to take it. "Awesome," I said. "Thanks, Rhys."

His eyes flicked up at me as that little smile curved his lips. Then they flicked back down. He was taking off his gloves, tossing them into the garbage can, and pulling on a fresh pair.

I smiled down at my beautiful serving of ice cream art, and then up at my dad. He kissed the top of my head.

# 22

I REALLY WANTED to get to school early, but it took Mom forever to drag Danny out of bed. I think she might have been actually brushing his teeth as he stood there in his pajamas; I don't know, don't want to. I waited in the car.

"I have to—"

"I *know*, Niki," Mom said, pulling backward down the driveway. "I know, okay? I have things today too, I have a house that needs more than . . ." She stopped. "It's fine, everything's fine!"

I turned to Danny. "Dude," I said. "You have to get yourself up in the mornings. You're not a baby. You're nine now."

He growled at me.

"Niki," Mom said.

I looked out the window. *Niki? How is this on ME?*

"Your glasses look so cute," she said, glancing at me in the rearview.

I didn't say anything.

"Everybody's gonna love them," she said. "I know it can feel stressful, going to school with a new—"

"That's not why I'm stressed," I said.

"You seem a little stressed," she said, with a pleading giggle in her voice. But I wasn't in the mood.

"I get marked down for being late," I mumbled. "I can't—I can't be late every day."

"You'll be there before the bell," Mom said, gliding through the stop sign.

The car was barely stopped when I opened the door and got out. I heard her yelling to me to have a good day. I didn't thank her or wish her a good day back, which I know is so rude and would gnaw at me the rest of the day, but right then I didn't care. I was rushing to get in. Danny hadn't even unbuckled his seat belt.

It's true, the bell hadn't rung yet.

We Are All Friends Here on the sign over my head. Wow, you can see the ridges in the paint strokes on the letters. The diamond sparkles of the treads on the steps. I held the banister going up.

The thing is, as much as it was cool to see everything in high definition, it also (I know this isn't true, but this is how it felt right at that moment) felt like suddenly everybody would be able to see me more clearly too. Like I'd shrugged off my superpower of blurriness. Like I was strutting up into the eighth-grade hallway like the star of a music video, in four-inch heels, a gold bodysuit, and fake eyelashes, singing

HERE I AM at top volume. Even though I was in my jeans and boots and cozy blue sweatshirt.

I peered around the stairwell barrier to the eighth-grade area.

The only people *not* watching the Squad (plus Ava) practice cartwheels were Holly, Beth, and Nadine. They were sitting on the floor, chattering away. Everybody else was watching the Squad like they were a live show of celebrities. Ava fit in perfectly, I had to admit that to myself. She looked like she was having genuine fun with them. Not annoyed, not tense. Just relaxed and, well, happy.

"Niki!"

I turned. Holly was waving.

"Hi." I waved back. Holly smiled and wiggled over to make room for me. *Okay, then,* I decided. *Guess that's the only place for me. On the floor, with the unpopular kids,* I thought, nastily.

"I love your new glasses, Niki," Holly said as soon as I got close.

I pushed them up my nose. "Thanks," I said.

"They look great," she said. "How do they see?"

I laughed, sitting down. "Great," I said. "Everything is so . . . specific."

"Isn't that a mind-quake?"

"Yes!"

Holly was smiling her gentle smile back at me. She pushed her glasses up at the exact same time as I did the same thing. We tilted our heads to the side and laughed one burble of HA! in unison.

"Remember when your mom used to call us Frick and Frack?" Holly asked.

"Yes!"

"And sometimes one of us would say *Hi, Frick* and the other would say *Hi, Frack*?"

"Which was which?" Nadine asked.

"It didn't matter," I said. "I remember that. Hi, Frick!"

"Hi, Frack," Holly said.

"But what does that mean?" Beth asked. "Is it from, like, a TV show or something?"

"No idea," Holly and I both said.

"Jinx!" Beth yelled.

"Holly Jasper Jones," Nadine said. "I don't know your middle name, Niki."

"Pickle!" Holly said.

"Pickle?" Nadine asked. "Seriously? Because if so, Niki, that is the coolest thing I ever heard."

Holly and I glanced at each other. "No," I admitted. "It's Patrice, which I hated when I was little, so Holly and I decided to change it to Pickle. We thought pickles were the most sophisticated food and we liked them, so we figured we were all that."

"Amazing," Beth said.

"Pickles *are* very sophisticated," Nadine agreed. "Especially for kindergartners. You were so right."

"I'm changing my middle name to Sauerkraut," Beth said.

"You like sauerkraut?" Nadine asked her.

"No," Beth said as the bell rang. "But a girl can dream."

"Ambition is important," Holly said.

"The most sophisticated thing I like is, I guess, cake," Nadine said.

"Awesome middle name," I said. "Nadine Cake Green?"

"I love it," Nadine said. "It's a lot nicer than Edna. I don't think my dead great-grandmother Edna would mind, do you?"

I laughed. "I think she'd be honored."

"Me too," said Holly.

They waited while I shoved my scooter into my locker, and walked in a clump around me to first period. Nobody was rolling their eyes that I said *honored*, or was slow, or that my locker was a disaster.

It was nice.

But in the math classroom, my sneakers were waiting neatly, all sparkling clean, on top of my desk. I turned to thank Ava for bringing them for me. She wasn't in her seat.

Ava was sitting on Chase Croft's desk, and Britney was on Milo's. They were both leaning back on their arms, whispering to each other in their matching flowy tops. And nobody, glasses or not, could take their eyes off them.

# 23

"HAVE SOME MEAT," Dad said, again.

"No, thanks," I said. *Please let me just get through this dinner and up to my room; why does everyplace have to be a test?*

"You can't just eat starch," he said.

"Have three bites," Mom tried, like I was a little kid.

I am thirteen, almost fourteen. Not six.

"No commenting on other people's food choices," I said.

"Niki," Mom said. "Fine. Let's just have a pleasant dinner, okay?"

Danny was happily chomping away at his steak.

"I made the steak on the grill," Dad said. "It's expensive."

"More for you, then," I tried.

"I got enough for the *family*," Dad said.

"Jake," Mom said. "It's okay. You like it, Danny?"

"It's a little too rare," Danny said, with his mouth full. "I like it pink, not red on the inside. Dad likes it still mooing."

That's the joke Dad always makes, when we are at a restaurant. *Still mooing.*

*Dead cow dead cow still mooing* rattled around in my brain.

*They're just stressed because of Danny's testing tomorrow,* I told myself. *The cow is already dead. Not mooing. Maybe I should just eat it.* I looked at the pile of meat on the serving plate.

"I'm eating the broccoli and the carrots, too," I argued instead of giving in. "Not just starch."

"You need protein," Dad said.

"One slice?" Mom asked.

"No, thanks," I said.

Dad jabbed a fork into three slices of meat and flung them onto my plate.

*The wet slap of the meat onto the plate*

*The red bleeding out from the slices into my mashed potatoes*

*IT'S MY PLATE EWWWW*

I jolted my plate up, away from me, and dumped my food onto the table.

We all went silent.

I had never done anything like that before.

My dinner was all over the table and my stained plate lay empty in front of me.

I put my hands in my lap and stared at the table.

I never even had tantrums when I was little. That was Danny's job. I always did what I was supposed to. Obedience is *my* superpower. Also my weakness.

Nobody moved as the meat juice spread across the table

and dripped off. Well, nobody but Fumble, who happily lapped up the puddle.

I was at least as shocked at what had just happened as any of them, and they all had their mouths wide open. Me too. I closed mine. Closed my eyes, to stop seeing the mess I'd made of the table and also to brace for what was about to happen to me. Mom hates messes.

"Jake!" Mom yelled just as I was opening my mouth to say *sorry sorry sorry.*

We all turned to look at her. *What?*

"Me?" Dad asked. "She just . . ."

"She said no thank you!"

"She—"

"She said she didn't want it."

"That doesn't excuse—"

"She said no," Mom said. "No means no. Not everybody wants the same things. Niki, you may get a fresh plate. Let's clean this up, Jake."

I went over to the cabinet and got a fresh plate while Dad, beside me, got the paper towels. Fumble was enthusiastically licking the floor. Dad went back to the table and used huge wads of paper towels to clean up the mess I'd made. He dumped handfuls of paper towels full of my ex-dinner into the trash can, which Mom had brought over next to the table. Mom served me fresh mashed potatoes and vegetables on my new plate. All in silence.

The rest of dinner, no talking. Silverware clanked on

plates, everybody stared at the table, nobody talked until Danny said, "Can I have more steak?"

Dad served him the last four slices.

"May I be excused?" I asked.

"Yes," Mom said. "Please help clear."

Dad took his plate to the sink and started washing the dishes, his broad back to us.

# 24

I WENT UPSTAIRS as soon as I could, straight to my room. It had been such a weird dinner, I felt like I had to tell somebody about it. But it was not the kind of thing I could text to Ava, was it? Nobody else really knows about my crazy family, though.

My brain was whirling like a potter's wheel, swirling around so lurchingly, I couldn't latch down any single thought long enough to think it. How to slow it down enough to get my feet solid on the floor?

Maybe I could tell Holly?

**Hi Holly it's Niki guess what I did tonight, I dumped my dinner off my plate!**

Yeah, no. Weird. Delete. Before I hit send! Yay me!

Maybe I could text Milo. We're friends. No reason to be . . .

Hahahaha. As if. Didn't even type one word. Turned off my phone to stop myself.

Science test tomorrow. Maybe instead of worrying about popularity or what Milo meant when he said today, in the hallway before social studies, "I like your glasses," I could focus on doing well in school. Get straight As. I'm wholesome and bookish? Fine. Lean in to that.

Just because Mom thinks friendship is the most important thing doesn't mean I do. I can be independent and strong. A loner. If I am brilliant at science, maybe I could really become a meteorologist as famous and popular as Breezy Khan.

Certain people will be sorry they dumped me back in eighth grade, if that happens.

I opened the boring science textbook to chapter three and read:

> The **bedrock** of Maine is creased with fault lines. **Fault lines** are breaks in the **earth** where rock has moved. Fault lines are typically where **earthquake** activity occurs. But the fault lines in Maine are older, are not geologically active, and do not move the way the younger, more active fault lines do.
>
> The fault lines in Maine have little to do with the earthquakes that occur in Maine.

Earthquakes? We have EARTHQUAKES?

I turned my phone back on, just in case anybody might have an emergency and need to reach me. To my surprise, it buzzed right away. Holly had just texted me: **Have you read the science homework yet? We have EARTHQUAKES in Maine?**

I had to smile. Frick and Frack. I started texting: **I was just thinking that exact**

Mom was walking past my room, on her way to Danny's, but stopped. "What's so funny?" she asked.

"What do you mean?" I asked.

"You look—happy," she said.

I shrugged. "Just texting with friends."

Mom smiled a big, real smile. "Hi, Ava!" she said.

I didn't correct her.

She went on to Danny's room.

I picked up my phone again. Texted back to Holly: **I was just thinking that exact thing! This is why we probably shouldn't do the reading—tooo stressful!!!**

Holly texted back **ahahahahahaha.**

I hearted that because what is there to say in response?

Then I texted **Hey** to Ava, and hit send.

Just *hey.*

*Hey* isn't weird. Nothing wrong with texting *hey*. We're still supposedly friends, just not hanging out together at school so much.

No response.

Whatever. Focus on studying. Bedrock. Folk rock. Bedrock. Bed.

Still no text back from Ava. Fine. Maybe *hey* is too nothing.

I erased my notes in my notebook, which to be fair were basically just some names in cursive (*Ava Milo Holly Britney*

*Milo*) and the word *if.* I like to write the word *if* in cursive. I like how it flows. *ifififififif*

> *IF*
>
> *A new poem by Niki Ames*
>
> *ififififififififif*

I drew abstract lines radiating out from it and then erased them. Erased the whole page. Holly is good at art. I am not good at art. I am good at:

1. Erasing
2.

I typed and deleted, typed and deleted a second text to Ava:

**I'm sorry**

**Hey I might have a crush on somebody and need some flirting tips!**

**Please don't be mad at**

**You should've been here tonight dinner with the Ames fam was INSANE and it was ME who was the crazy person for**

**I thought of someone to maybe have a crush on**

**Did you see there's a storm coming beginning of next week**

**Hey do you think school will be canceled if Hurric**

**My brother is so**

**Please**

DELETE DELETE DELETE.

Mom was trying to persuade Danny to do his homework.

He grunted at her.

She said, "I don't like that kind of response, Danny."

"Don't touch my stuff!" he yelled at her.

Something crashed.

*Oh no, not this*, I thought. *Not the Dance. I hate the Dance.*

"Don't! Touch! My! Stuff!!!!"

I should research earthquakes on the internet probably, so I'll be able to add in some interesting details on the test tomorrow, get some extra credit maybe, instead of watching the Dance unfold, as, uh-oh, ayuh, there goes Mom, scurrying away from Danny's room. Stuff is crashing— books, games, the game ball. Everything is smashing into the walls.

Fumble ran into my room, ears flattened to his head, and jumped up on the bed next to me. "Same bet?" I asked him.

Countdown to Dad stomping toward Danny's room starting now: 10, 9, 8 . . .

There's a thing in weather called a barometer, which measures atmospheric pressure. I don't know how they measure that; maybe I will research that now because, 4, 3, yes, here's Dad!

Between my phone not getting any response texts and Dad yelling at Danny to *Listen to your mother*, the atmospheric pressure in my house would break even the toughest barometer if we had one.

*BOOM!* The storm was raging in my brother's room.

*Wham*—something hit the wall that separates our rooms so hard, the picture of me and Ava from July, arms around each other at the beach, popped off and hit the floor.

I slipped off the bed and picked it up. There was a crack in the glass. I ran my thumb along it. Got a tiny cut.

*Stop it, stop it!* Mom yelled. At Dad or Danny? Hard to tell.

"Danny!" Dad thundered.

"Get out! Get out of my room!" Danny raged.

"Clean this up NOW!" Dad yelled.

I flattened myself against the wall, holding the cracked picture, sucking my bleeding thumb. *I win this time*, I whispered to Fumble. *Yayyyy, hooray. Hooray for me.*

"Jake!" Mom yelled.

Dad stomped out.

I heard him as he passed my door in the hall, growling, "I am so sick of being the bad guy here."

The Dance. The usual. *It's fine, it's what happens, don't worry*, I reminded Fumble. I put my earbuds in and blasted some music. Whatever. I just wanted to think about something else, escape this all for a little while. Math. At least there are answers, one right answer for each and every problem.

More crashes from next door. Volume up, math book open, sitting on the floor of my closet.

I was getting a headache from my earbuds and every song felt too much like commentary on my actual life, plus still no texts, so I turned off my phone. Which left me in the dark, with no more music. I pulled out my eraser and imagined, what if I were a math genius, or a writer, or an artist, and I could just make amazing things come out every time I wrote them, in ink, and I never felt the urge to erase a thing because everything worked? Right away, first try.

*SMASH.*

My mother hates messes, hates when I write on my sneakers but tough, *CRASH* I wrote on them anyway. *If If If If,* I wrote, marring their newly clean sides.

*If* is what I wrote but not what I was thinking, which was:

*I like the feel and the sound of my erasable blue ballpoint pen gliding on my sneaker's rubber side-sole. I don't like hearing my brother cry, or, gods please forgive me, the sound of my mother consoling him.*

# 25

THE SCIENCE TEST was fine. Ms. Finch said that after we turned in our papers, we could do whatever we wanted.

*I would like to move to the Bahamas, in that case, please,* I thought on my way back to my seat.

I glanced around the room. Madeleine was hunched over her paper, still writing and writing. Britney was making funny, panicked faces at everybody. Ava, her finished paper still on her desk, was pretending to cough but was actually laughing.

Milo, walking past me to hand in his paper, bumped my chair with his foot. It startled me so much in the quiet of the room, I jumped.

"Sorry!" he whispered.

"It's okay," I said.

My eyelashes kept tapping the lenses of my glasses with every blink. Maybe mascara isn't worth it if you have glasses, I don't know. Mom had forgotten about buying me the hypoallergenic kind, so, good thing I stole her old one. I wasn't mad, of course. She had bigger problems than my eyelashes to worry about. Testing tomorrow.

In gym, Ms. Andry said, "Stand with your best friend."

I was next to Holly, Nadine, and Beth already. Holly and I shrugged at each other and it was fine, fun, playing catch with weighted balls. Each catch was a thud in our arms, and took both hands.

"I try to play catch with Danny," I told her, after I almost bobbled a catch. "But he always ends up not wanting to throw the ball back to me. He wants to pretend it's a pizza or a cake and have a party with it instead." I heaved the ball at her.

"Ugh," Holly said, catching it. "I love it. A cake?"

"Seriously?" Nadine said. "Turn all the balls into cakes? He's got my vote."

"It's interesting," Milo said, behind me. "Like instead of goodbye, it's cake!"

"Goodbye?" I asked.

Milo was blushing. "Catch is stressful!"

"To you?" I asked. "You always play catch."

"And it's always stressful!" Milo said. "You want the ball, right? That's the point. You're like, Here! Here! Throw it to me! But when you get it? You don't get to keep it. Right away, you're supposed to throw it back. All those goodbyes . . ."

"I never thought of it like—"

"Hey!" Ms. Andry said. "Did I say it's time to chat? No, I did not. No chatting!"

Milo never gets in trouble with teachers either. We turned back to our partners.

When the bell rang and we were putting the weighted balls away, Holly said, "Let's eat lunch outside today, yeah? With everybody. It's a nice day."

"Okay," I said.

"You're smiling like the cat who ate the canary."

"The what?" I asked. "Ew! Why would the cat do that?"

But she was right. I was smiling. It felt nice on my face.

It wasn't till we were on our way out that I realized I hadn't even been watching the Squad out of the corners of my eyes, that whole time.

# 26

"GUESS I'LL RIDE my bike to school," I told Mom in the morning.

"What?" she asked. "I thought you hated your bike."

"I just, I know you have a lot to deal with today," I said.

She looked up from the Cream of Wheat she was making for Danny.

"It's okay. He'll be okay, whatever happens," I said.

"I just don't want him to feel like there's something wrong with him," Mom whispered.

"But what if there is?" I asked.

"What? There is nothing wrong with him, Niki."

"I know. But if there is, I'm just saying *if.* Maybe they could find it and help . . ."

"Don't. You. Dare. He is my CHILD."

"I'm aware."

Her eyes opened wider.

"Sorry," I said quickly. "I was trying to be supportive. Sorry."

"I don't want him to feel judged," Mom said.

"I know."

"Sorry," she said. "I don't mean to take it out on you. I'm a little tense."

"I know. It's okay," I told her. "I am too. I was trying to reassure you. Sorry."

She held out her non-stirring arm to me. "You're the finest kind, Niki."

I stepped close and let myself be folded into her hug. "You are, Mom."

The Cream of Wheat smelled good, buttery. But I wanted to get going before Danny came down, and if I'm completely honest, I wanted to not run the risk of Milo or Robby seeing me wobble on my bike. They ride every day, and I, well, don't.

I got my bike out of the garage. *I can do this*, I told myself.

I unlooped the helmet from the handlebars and smooshed it onto my head, readjusted my glasses, which I had knocked half off, and tightened my backpack straps. *It's like riding a bike*, I reminded myself as I wheeled it out to my driveway.

"Niki!" Robby yelled from next door.

"You riding to school?" Milo asked.

"No," I said.

"What are you doing, then?" Robby asked.

I looked down at my bike. The loose straps of the helmet swung beside my cheeks. "I am, obviously, posing for a fashion shoot."

"Obviously," Milo said.

"Should we wait for you?" Robby asked.

"Hundred percent no," I said. "I have to remember how to work this thing and it could take a minute. Hour. Month."

"Come on, Milo," Robby said.

"You sure?" Milo said. "I could mansplain where the pedals are to you."

"Thanks," I said. "But there can be no witnesses to this fiasco."

"Okay," Milo said. Milo just rode off normally, but Robby somehow swung his leg straight behind him and over the bike while it was already moving. Just watching that made me drop my bike and scrape my ankle with it.

Maybe Robby is actually the cuter one?

I heard commotion behind me in the house. *Gotta go*, I thought.

I picked up my bike. *Pretend you can do it*, I told myself. I straddled the bike and pushed off. Wobbly but okay. One reason I hate riding my bike is my bumpy dirt road. *Okay, okay*, I sang quietly to myself as I pedaled. It's the song Mom used to sing to me and to Danny when we were little and upset. *Okay* is the only lyric, and she would sing it over and over until I (or, much more often, Danny) calmed down, and then sit there in the silence afterward with us.

*Okay, okay, okay*, I sang to myself, all the way to Victory Boulevard. Didn't fall. *Okay*. And then rode in the silence of just the wind in my ears the rest of the way to school.

As I locked up at the bike rack, Milo said, "You made it!"

I laughed. "Just barely!"

"Hi, Niki," Isabel said. "See you soon!" She turned and caught up to the rest of the Squad before I managed a hello in return.

I took off my helmet. "Is my hair ridiculous?" I asked Milo.

"No, it's pretty."

Well, neither of us knew what to do about that. I took off my backpack and put it back on.

"I gotta . . ." he said.

"Yeah," I said.

He ran into school. I watched. What was that? I was rooted to the spot.

"You okay?" Holly asked, coming up behind me.

"What? Yes. No. Fine."

"Just guarding the bikes today? Or, are you coming into school?"

"Right, yes."

We walked together toward the front doors.

"We are all friends here," I said as we passed under the sign.

"Whether we like it or not," Holly said.

# 27

WE HAD TO go collect our pots from the table, when we got to art class. Some kids had etched designs into theirs, or carved their names. Some were super smooth and shaped all curvy. Mine was, well . . .

"I like how you left your fingerprints all over yours," Holly said, beside me. "And that sticky-outy bit. Is cool. Is that, is it a . . . Is that X-rated?"

I laughed. "It was supposed to be an elephant."

"And that's his . . ."

"Trunk!" We were both laughing. "And those are his ears! See?"

"Oh! Okay, yeah."

I looked at hers. It was graceful. Wide, then narrow, then wide again. Smooth all over. "Holy—Holly, that's gorgeous."

"Thanks," Holly said, and didn't argue that no, no, it was bad, see these faults, awful. She turned it in her hands and looked at it. "I was thinking about calla lilies."

We took our containers to our table. We had to write our names on the bottoms and anything else we wanted to write, maybe the date, or who they were a gift for. They'd go in the kiln before our next class.

Who mine was a gift for? My mom, I guess. Mom and Dad?

Danny? Like me, he was a single elephant, empty and alone.

He'd just break it.

*Niki Ames*, I wrote. *3rd Elephant.*

I set it down on the table. Nadine and Beth were chatting, but Holly was just looking out the window. Milo was concentrating very hard on whatever he was writing on the underside of his bowl, his lips pressed between his teeth, which must've hurt, with his braces and everything. I checked the clock: 11:11. Make a wish.

*I wish Danny would do well on his test.*

*I wish they will find whatever is wrong with him and*

*I wish Danny*

"You okay?" Holly was asking, her hand on my arm.

I smiled, or tried. It didn't fully work.

"Tell me at lunch," she said.

So at lunch, in the library, I did. I told her that Danny had thrown a fit, and possibly a book, and that he has tantrums at home, and my parents end up fighting, and I worry they'll get divorced, and if they do, I will never forgive Danny. I even told her the worst stuff, like sometimes I wish Danny were deaf or blind or had a limp, something visible, so that people would know there was really something wrong and my parents couldn't deny it and people like Ava's mom, Samantha, wouldn't say to my mom, *Maybe you should tell him not to act that way*, or, *Maybe he should do more sports so he won't be so coddled and he'll learn to be more rough-and-tumble? That's all he really needs.*

Because when I hear Samantha say stuff like that to my mom, it makes me want to punch her in her big white teeth. *My mom makes him play Little League and it is a massive honking chore, Samantha! And it doesn't heal him at all.*

Nothing does.

Nothing cures him.

But I feel like I am being a crappy sister and a crappy daughter, that I am wishing that the testing shows *something* and maybe that is what I am, maybe I just fully suck. But if Danny were deaf, people wouldn't be yelling at him, *Why aren't you listening?* because if they did, *they'd* be the ridiculous, stupid jerks. If he were deaf, we'd all learn sign language. And other kids in his class would too. Or maybe he'd get a cochlear implant and we'd video him hearing us tell him we love him for the first time, and everybody would cry and realize how awesome he is. If he were blind, we'd get a Seeing Eye dog and people would take turns reading his homework to him, like Isabel had offered me. But the thing that's wrong with Danny is more like, he wants friends but doesn't know how to navigate that, and he doesn't handle his own feelings particularly well, and so everybody finds him annoying.

Including, horribly, sometimes: me.

But maybe there is a cure, or help, or a way to teach him, and they could find it, they could figure it out, and he'd get better.

Or at least people would understand. Maybe there would be space for him to just be Danny, if the way he is is just the way he is, not because he's a brat or because he or my parents are doing it wrong.

"Sorry," I finally said, wiping the tears off my face. "I've been talking for a half hour straight, pouring all my garbage out on your head. Sorry."

"Don't," Holly said. "You can just, you don't have to apologize. I'm your friend."

"You are," I said. "Thank you."

"You can just tell me how awesome I am, if you need to say something."

"You're better than a Fisherman's Friend."

"And even more powerful."

"But less disgusting."

"Thank you," Holly said.

"I fully thought you were offering me a magical little fairy, the first time you gave me one of those lozenges, by the way."

"Who says I wasn't?" Holly asked, with that twinkle in

her eyes, and then got serious. "Niki. Danny's lucky to have you as his sister."

I shook my head. "No, he's not."

"He is. And he's right to love you."

"Not really."

"This is hard on all of you. But you see him. That's not nothing. And you love him."

"I do," I said. "But I'm not, I don't—I wish I could help him, but I don't think doing his homework for him is actually . . ."

"Let's send him good, strong thoughts, to be his true self during the testing."

"Okay," I said. I took off my glasses. "That's the wish I was searching for."

She closed her eyes. I closed mine, too, and made the wish. *Be you, Danny. Just be you. That's all you need to be. And then if you need help, the universe—or I—will figure out how to get it to you. Please let that be true.*

I opened my eyes. Holly was looking at me, full of solemn caring.

"He'll be okay," she whispered.

"I hope so," I said.

The bell rang. We hadn't even started our sandwiches. I managed not to apologize. We shrugged at each other and shoved sandwiches into our mouths as we walked. "Cheese and pickles for the win," Holly said. "Want a taste?"

I took a bite of her sandwich. "Yum! I love pickles."

"I remember."

I took a bite of my cheddar-cheese-without-pickles sandwich. "Hey," I said on our way down the hall. "You want to sleep over Saturday night?"

"I thought you don't . . ."

I shrugged. "It would be really fun, if you could."

"I'd love to," Holly said, handing me her sandwich for another bite.

My face was probably all red, but I didn't even care. We went together to fifth period and I felt, honestly, beautiful.

# 28

DANNY WAS WATCHING his shows when I got home. "I told him he could watch as much as he wants tonight," Mom said quickly when she saw me looking at him.

"Okay," I said.

"He had his testing."

"How did it go?"

"Beats me," Mom said. "So far, he's said, *Fine*, and *Can I watch my shows?* So."

I nodded. "Sounds about right."

I went up to do my homework and did some group-texting with Holly, Nadine, and Beth about if you could go to any time in a time machine but just for three hours, and you'd be fully safe but could do any one action, what would you do?

In the middle of it, Isabel texted me: **How's everything going?**

**Good**, I texted back. **How 'bout you?**

**Amazing!** Isabel texted.

I didn't know what to make of that, so I hearted it and got back into the debate about imaginary time-travel dilemmas while simultaneously doing my homework.

Dad called me to come for dinner. My name in his voice sounded loud and sudden, accusatory. I washed my hands and went down to the kitchen, prepared to deal with slabs of meat and the fight that would come. Boy, my parents sure won the parenting lottery.

Dad had made pasta with butter and sage from our garden. "No meat at all," he told me proudly. "And for you, Danny? Hamburgers!"

He put one on Danny's plate. Well done, no ketchup or other toppings. Just how he likes it.

I took a bite of the pasta. It was really good. Plus, I appreciated that Dad had clearly wanted to make something special for me, when here it should be a night all about Danny. I wanted to say thank you for that, but then it felt weird to. Making a thing of it. I decided to compliment it, figuring that would get it across. "This is—"

"We should watch the news later," Dad said at the same time.

"Sorry, what?" I said.

"What?" Dad also said.

"Delicious," I said as he said, "The storm."

"Right. Hurricane Oliana," Mom said. "Looks like we could be in the bull's-eye."

"It's destroying parts of Florida," Danny said with a mouth full of hamburger.

"Oh," I said. "Hey. Did you know there are sometimes earthquakes in Maine?"

"Really?" Mom asked. "That's scary. Real earthquakes?"

"According to my science textbook."

"I thought those earthquakes were just me," Danny said. "Throwing all my stuff around my room."

I laughed. He had never joked about having a tantrum before. We honestly never really discussed his tantrums. We're all always like, *Well, that was horrible. Hopefully that'll never happen again. Never mention. Say nothing, say nothing.*

Mom and Dad were staring at Danny.

"You guys have no sense of humor," Danny said. "That was a joke. Because obviously I know it's not an earthquake when I throw my own things. An earthquake starts far below the earth's surface. Only Niki and I have a sense of humor in this family. I don't know where we got it."

I took the opportunity to look at Danny, actually look at him, for the first time through my new glasses. Does he look strange? Like someone who should be *labeled*?

He just looked like Danny. I mean, sunglasses inside, slightly messy hair standing up in points, rosy cheeks. But, just like he always looked. Hard to say if he looks like me. I tried to picture myself and couldn't even do that. Maybe, despite my glasses, I still don't see well.

"There's less than a five-percent chance of a hurricane ever making a direct hit on Snug Island," Danny said.

"Oh, that's good news!" Mom said.

"But the riptides are going to be very intense all

weekend," he said, with burger half-chewed in his mouth.

"Yeah," Dad agreed. "Good point, Danny. Lots of activity down at the marina today, everybody starting to secure the boats ahead of it."

"The Tobins must be going nuts," Mom said. "This kind of thing wreaks havoc on their pots. Oh, I should go by and check on that house I have listed on the water, make sure the—"

"If you get caught in a riptide," Danny interrupted, "you shouldn't fight it. Swim across it. Forty percent of drownings are due to fighting a riptide."

Why does he so annoy me, so fast, just when I'm fully on his side? It boils my insides when he acts like an expert on stuff he doesn't know about. I mean, forty percent? How would anyone even know that? How can they be sure the people didn't get a cramp? I mean, yes, I learned it every spring in school, too, that if you're caught in an undertow or riptide, don't try to swim back to shore or fight it, don't panic or give up. Swim parallel to the beach. *WE ALL KNOW.* But he presents things like they're new, brilliant ideas he just thought of himself, and adds fake facts as if he's an expert.

*Be kind*, I told myself. *Be the finest kind.*

"Exactly," I agreed. "Don't panic, right? But also, don't give up and get pulled out to sea, even if it feels like, oh, the ocean is choosing me . . ."

"The ocean isn't choosing anything," Danny said.

"No," I agreed. "I know. I was just kidding."

"I don't get the joke," Danny said. "Oceans don't make choices."

"I just, I, never mind," I said.

Mom and Dad were watching us, frowning.

"Maybe I'm the only one in the family with a sense of humor," Danny said.

After dinner, I stopped in Danny's room.

"That was funny," I said.

"Yeah," he agreed. "The joke I made, but not your joke. A joke has to be funny or it's just a sentence."

"Good point."

"You taught me that."

"I did?"

"Yeah, remember?"

I shook my head.

"When those boys were making fun of me in second grade, when we had to play musical chairs and I cried. You said you hated them because they were mean to me."

"I did," I said. "I do."

"I know," Danny said. "But I was standing up for them, because they kept saying, 'It's just a joke,' and 'Can't you take a joke?'"

"I do vaguely remember that," I said. "They were mean to you and then trying to make it like it was your fault for not liking it. Pissants."

"And you said, 'It's not a joke, Danny. A joke has to be funny or it's just a sentence.'"

"Okay."

"I always remember that one," Danny said. "I have an excellent memory."

"How did the testing go today?" I asked.

"Fine," he said.

"Do you . . . Danny? Can I, Danny, can I ask you something?"

"That was a question, so obviously yes."

I walked into his room and sat on his bed. "Why did you get tested today?" I asked him. "Why did they want to do testing, on you? Any idea?"

He kept playing his game. I couldn't really see his eyes through his sunglasses.

"Danny?"

"I'm thinking."

"Okay."

I sat there for a while. Just when I was about to stand up and say, *Forget it,* he said, "I think it was because I went to the coat closet during the social studies test."

"You . . . what?"

"I have a key to the house, now that I'm in fourth grade. Dad got it made for me, and I have to not lose it. I was thinking about my key. I was thinking, *Is my key in the pocket of my coat?* So, I went to check. And then she yelled at me."

"Ms. Broderick?"

"Yeah. But I needed my key, or to make sure it was there, because I'm supposed to not lose it, and she was saying *Danny Danny Danny* at me and a lot of other yelling, so I sat down to wait."

"Wait for what?"

"For her to finish saying *Danny Danny Danny.* That's what

I always wish when people say *Danny* . . ."

"What do you wish?"

"I wish they would stop saying DANNY. Or that my name could be Tom."

Where to even start with him? "Danny, you can't go to the closet during a test—maybe she thought you were cheating."

"I wasn't."

"I know that. I know you wouldn't. But how would Ms. Broderick know whether you were looking at answers in your coat or something?"

"I wasn't cheating," Danny said. "I was looking for my key. I told you."

"Yeah," I said. "I heard—did you also throw a book?"

"That was a different time."

"Right. You threw a book at Ms. Broderick?"

"No."

"No?"

"I just threw it. Not *at* her."

"But it hit her?"

He didn't answer.

"Did you yell *I don't want you* at Margot Hu?"

"Yeah."

"Why? Danny!"

"I didn't want her."

"How do you think that made her feel, you yelling that?"

"I don't know." He looked perplexed at the question, like it was the weirdest thing I could ask. "She didn't say anything about her feelings. She walked away."

"Okay," I said. "Anyway, the testing was okay?"

I waited while he thought. After a long minute, he said, "The questions she asked were interesting, and she let me tell my full thoughts without interrupting me, which Mom and Dad don't do. Which they should do, for me. Because I might have some differences in how my brain works. Therefore, my eyes are more sensitive to light. My kind of brain might be the kind that makes me great at noticing and remembering details, but not as smooth at friendship as some people are."

I waited, making sure he was done.

He was staring at me, his expression blank.

"So, you feel okay about it?"

He shrugged. "It feels good to know maybe there is something real that is different about me. Something interesting. That I'm not just stupid or lazy."

"Did somebody call you those things?" I asked, my hand tightening into a fist.

"However," Danny insisted. "Mom said not to think of it as having a disability. If I have that kind of brain. She said to think of it as maybe having some gifts, and also some challenges to overcome, like everybody has."

"That makes sense," I said.

"Everybody has gifts and challenges."

"Okay."

"I have sensitive ears, too. I scored the highest of anyone ever on my hearing test."

"I know it."

"Have you heard of body language?"

"Sure," I said. "Why?"

"The psychologist was asking me about body language. I thought she meant the game show. You know that show? On YouTube?"

"No," I said.

"I said, Okay, I'll watch it again, and she asked, What? She didn't know what I meant. I've watched all seven seasons."

"Danny, I think maybe she meant—"

"I wanted to talk about the show, but she said I could tell her about it a different time, maybe next week. This week she wanted to say that body language is also a way that people communicate but not with words. You have to look right at people and see what they are communicating with their face and body. Did you know that?"

"I guess," I said. "I mean, sure."

"So then you're probably not on the spectrum," he said. "I might be."

"Okay."

"That's what it's called, the kind of brain I might have, but we don't know yet. Things other people just seem to know, I have to learn. But everybody has to pay attention to body language. It's not easy for anybody, but it may be harder for some people, like me. Maybe. If I have that. I have to make sure I'm looking at people to see what they're saying, with body language. You can find out their secret feelings, with that technique."

"Okay."

He stared at me. "I can't tell what you're feeling. I just see you sitting on my bed."

"I feel . . ." I said. "I feel like, I guess, like, I hope you feel okay about the testing."

"Oh."

"How are you feeling about it?"

He didn't answer.

"Danny?"

"Maybe you're on the spectrum too, because you don't know how I'm feeling."

"Danny, I don't . . ."

"I feel fine," he said. "I also feel a little hungry and a little sleepy and a little like playing some more of this game."

"Okay," I said, and left. I could hear his game beeping and blipping as I halfway shut his door, and then mine, behind me.

# 29

RIDING MY BIKE to school the next morning was less terrifying. I was actually thinking about other things as I coasted down the hill on Victory, not just *don't fall don't die don't fall don't die*. The things I was thinking were, in order:

1. This is actually kind of fun
2. And much faster than waiting in the back seat of the car for Danny to get shoved out of the house by Mom
3. Is that Milo and Robby at the stop sign?
4. Don't fall don't die don't fall don't die right in front of them

"Hey," Robby said.

My heart was pounding so hard from the effort at not falling not dying that any response was impossible.

"How'd you do on the science test?" Milo asked.

"Um, okay," I said. "You?"

"He got a ninety-nine and he's pissed," Robby said.

"I don't think you should get a point off for spelling on a science test," Milo argued.

"Well, I don't think you should get fifteen points off for making up facts," Robby said, shrugging. "I'm not arguing."

"Just mocking," I said.

"Yeah," Robby agreed. "You going to Isabel's tomorrow?"

"To . . . oh, to Isabel's?"

"For the party?" Robby asked. "Tomorrow night? I thought I heard you and Ava were going."

"Oh," I said. "That. Sure. I mean, no. I'm, I have other plans."

"You should come," Milo said. "If you want to, I mean."

"Yeah, I'm doing a thing; I have plans. With Holly. Jones."

"Oh," Robby said. "Are you going somewhere? I heard her parents go to concerts in Boston sometimes. Didn't her mom used to be in a band or something?"

"Yeah, I think so," Milo said.

"We should go, right?" I asked. "To school?"

"Ugh, again?" Robby asked. "We're constantly doing that."

"It's like a habit at this point," Milo said.

This time they both did that cool graceful flip of their long legs over the seat while already moving. I was still lining my pedals up just so, straddling my bike and praying not to topple over.

I made it to school, and made it through the day without crying or blurting out anything about the party the Squad was having that I was not, obviously, invited to. I felt as empty and misshapen as my sad elephant bowl, which had cracked in the kiln.

Holly said she knows a way to fix it. Like a cracked bowl matters. Like it's anything but a metaphor to (for) me at this point. "Great," I said. "Thanks."

"I'll show you next week, or at our sleepover tomorrow night!"

"Super," I said, and saw Milo look away.

After school Mom asked if I could come help her at her open house on Sunday.

"Sure," I said. "But, um, hey. Would it be okay if Holly Jones sleeps over tomorrow night?"

I still hadn't asked, and here it was, twenty-four hours before Holly was going to show up with her sleeping bag and her stuffed goose named Gander and her art case, ready for all the fun we'd spent the past few days planning. But I knew how Mom would respond. And I was right.

"Of course!" Mom said, hugely positive. "Any of your friends are welcome here, anytime! All of them, in fact!"

"Just Holly," I said.

"That's fine," Mom said, smiling big. "That's great!"

"I know, Mom. You don't have to reassure me so much."

"Oh, I didn't mean it that way. I love Holly!"

Right. It's just, Mom knows what's happening with Ava, knows Ava moved up socially and dumped me. Mom feels terrible for me, the way I feel for Danny. That made me feel so much worse.

"Great, thanks," I said.

"Wow, I haven't really seen much of Holly in so long. She must be so much more grown-up now."

"Yeah, well."

"Is she still so creative? I always thought of her as super creative. Like you! Your pictures from Danny's party were so—oh, remind me to tell you—I hope you don't mind if I shared them with—"

"It's okay," I said, just wanting out of the conversation.

"I'm sure nothing will come of it, but who knows! And Holly's mom, so talented. I should give her a call. I always liked her, too. Is Holly still wearing those thick glasses or has she gotten contacts yet?"

"Glasses," I said. "Like me."

"Oh, sure, but hers were really thick, right? Yours are so cute. I had thick ones like hers when I was little and I couldn't wait to get contacts!"

"Some people like glasses," I said, and opened the fridge. "Do we have anything to eat?"

"I'm going to the store. You want to go with me? We can pick some fun snacks for you and Holly to have, for tomorrow night. And if you want, she could come too, if you want to come help at my open house. You could be my helpers! If that would be fun. But if you stay up late watching movies, you could sleep in, and you could ride your bikes over, whenever you're ready. You've gotten so into riding your bike, it's like you're a real teenager all of a sudden!"

I resisted saying, *As opposed to a fake teenager? I AM THIR-TEEN!* I knew she was trying to be nice, she wasn't the one

I was actually mad at, and I shouldn't be a brat. So I went with her to the grocery store and picked out snacks and food to have with Holly for our awesome sleepover that we were going to have so much fun at! While all the cool kids in the whole grade were at a real-teenager party that I was totally not invited to, so what, who cares.

# 30

I WAS VIDEO chatting with Holly, making plans for her to come over later, when everything started breaking apart.

I had told her my mom was really looking forward to seeing her, in fact was so excited for the sleepover that she had splurged and bought us three different types of face masks to try, and a sample pack of nail polishes. Mom was so happy I was interested in nail polish. I'm not. But I'd rather have bought than shoplifted nail polish, and I was trying to stretch, to grow up. Of course I didn't tell that to Holly. I wouldn't tell her about Ava stealing. Ava may have dumped me, but even in my angriest, most hurt moments, which are, to be fair, most of my moments, I wouldn't tell people that Ava is an actual thief. If she got arrested, I would go and sit with her in jail or at the police station and she'd see what a good friend I really am, and she'd regret everything and beg me to forgive her. And I'd say, *There's nothing to forgive.* And then I would forgive her anyway.

But still, I haven't told anybody.

Holly was saying her mom had loaded up her bag with extra markers and X-Acto knives.

"X-Acto knives?" I asked.

"Are they allowed at your house?"

"I guess," I said. "Honestly it's never come up. What would a person do with X-Acto knives?"

"Cut stuff out," she said. "You know, like if we want to cut things out of magazines, to make a collage or something? Do you have magazines?"

"Sure," I said. "And catalogs? My mom gets a lot of catalogs."

"Perfect," she said. "We could make posters. New motto posters! Or just do the face masks and nails, like you were thinking. Does Danny still like dancing? We could do dances with him, if you want."

I had to laugh. Ava always ignores Danny, and wants to stay in my room with the door closed. "I don't know," I said. "He likes those, you know, the shows with singing competitions?"

"Oh, we could make one of those, and rig it so he ends up the big winner! Wouldn't that be fun? We could make him prizes? You're so lucky you have a little brother. I just have Jaydon and he's so serious, always studying or practicing piano."

Her older brother is serious but also seriously handsome and smart. He played a piano concert last year for the whole seventh and eighth grades, even though he was in eleventh grade. It was really good. "Jaydon is awesome," I was saying, when my cell phone buzzed. I picked it up. It was Ava, texting:

**Hey if I tell you a secret you have to promise not to tell anyone okay?**

I texted below where my computer's camera could see:
**Of course**

Holly went on, talking about her brother and how he was deciding if he wanted to go to a regular college and study math, or a music college and study piano, and what her parents thought about that. Meanwhile, Ava was texting me:

**What do you think about Chase Croft?**
**me: Ummm . . . I don't know. Why?**

She hadn't texted me in over a week.

**Ava: Don't you think he looked kinda cute yesterday?**
**me: no**
**Ava: you totally did, I could tell! in a knuckle-dragger Neanderthal way?**
**me: Is that a way a person can look cute?**

Chase? Really? Gross. He is the opposite of cute. Did Ava think I liked him? What was she getting at? He had asked me if he could see my math homework as we walked into class yesterday, and I hadn't really wanted to let him but she doesn't collect it anyway, so why should I be a jerk about it? I let him have a look. He thanked me. Maybe Ava and the Squad thought I liked him or something. Ew.

Holly had moved on to ideas for things we could bake

tonight. A much nicer topic. "We could do cookies," I suggested.

"Have you ever made molten chocolate cakes? They're so delicious and honestly not that challenging. We could make them for your whole family!"

"That sounds awesome," I said.

"Do you have ramekins?"

"Do we have *what*?"

I checked my phone. Ava had texted: **You have to admit Chase has a nice chin**

Chin? I don't know. His chin? I never actually thought about anyone's chin before. What are the qualities of a good chin? What does a chin even do? What would make it good? His chin???

"Ramekins," Holly was saying. "You know those single-serving high-sided bowl things? I'm pretty sure we have some, so if you don't, I could bring some."

"What do you think makes a chin a good chin?" I asked Holly.

"A chin?" Holly stopped to consider it. "I guess, maybe, clear differentiation from the neck?"

"Huh," I said. "I guess so."

"I never really thought about it before," she said.

"Me either," I said.

Chase Croft is a skinny bonehead in track pants.

I tried to picture him, his chin, his face. His head looks like a skull. You could put a line drawing of his actual face on a bottle of poison and people would know not to drink it.

"Now I'm trying to picture everybody's chin," Holly was saying.

"Me too!"

Holly brought her computer into the bathroom with her. "Chins are weird, man."

I felt mine with my hand. "Mine has an indent."

"A cleft," Holly said. "Like mine. I like those, don't you? About our chins?"

"I guess," I said. I took my computer into the bathroom to look at my chin in the mirror too.

Ava texted: **And his cheekbones? Like, in a rough way? A little, yk, dangerous?**

**Dangerous like tuberculosis**, I typed but then deleted.

**me: He definitely has sticky-outy cheekbones.**

**Ava: Right????**

**me: Why are you asking me about Chase's face?**

Holly asked if everything was okay. I looked up. "Yeah," I said. "Actually, can I call you back in a sec? I just have to, um, deal with a thing. . . ."

"Okay!" she said. "See if you have ramekins. Oh, and yeast! Otherwise I could bring some. Flatbread pizzas?"

"Amazing," I said.

As I hung up, my phone was going nuts in my hand.

**Ava: You should come to Isabel's tonight**

**We're having a little party**

**It'll be fun**

**I could use a true friend there as a wingman!**

Who can I trust but you????

Come on come

Ask your mom

I texted her back: **I have plans.**

In one sec, the three dots, and then the flood:

Ava: Come on, Niki

This will be more fun

Pleaseeeeee

I miss you

Come to the partyyyyyyy

# 31

I CLOSED MY door to call Holly back.

She answered on the first ring. "So? Do you have ramekins?"

"I didn't, Holly, I . . ."

"What's wrong?" she asked. "Did something happen?"

"No, I just, I . . ."

"You look like you're about to cry, Niki. What is it? We don't have to make molten chocolate cakes if you don't want to."

"No, that's not . . . Holly."

"What? You can tell me."

"I was just thinking, do you think, you can say no and it's fine, but, do you think we could reschedule our sleepover? Do it a different night?"

I tried to read her body language but couldn't. *Maybe I am not okay too.*

"Sure," she said, and put down whatever it was she'd been holding.

"That would be great," I said.

"Is it because of Danny?" she asked quietly. "I know you worry people will judge you if he has a tantrum or something, and you should know that I hundred percent would not judge you or him or anyone."

"I know that," I said.

"If you'd rather come here, for the sleepover, that would also be great. I'm sure my mom would say yes, I would just have to confirm, but—"

"No," I quickly said. "I mean, yeah, that *would* be great. Sometime. Just, maybe not tonight, if that's okay."

"Oh," Holly said. "Okay." I noticed that beside her on the bed were her sleeping bag, a tote with a stuffed goose sticking out of it, and an art case.

"Sorry," I said.

"Niki."

"I mean, thanks."

She tilted her head slightly and said, "Okay then, I guess." And she hung up.

# 32

"OH! REALLY? CANCELED?" Mom asked. "Is Holly okay?"

"Yeah," I said impatiently. "Anyway, since that's not happening, is it okay if I go to a party at Isabel's?"

"At Isabel's?"

"Yeah."

"When were you invited to that?"

"Mom!" I yelled. "What is the difference? Can I go or not?"

"Niki. It's fine if you want to go to Isabel's, yes. That sounds fun."

I turned around to go upstairs and get ready.

"You want to talk about what's going on?"

"Nothing!"

She probably already knew about Isabel's party, of course, and that I wasn't invited. She probably figured out that I blew off Holly as soon as I got a better offer, and thinks I'm a terrible person, a horrible friend. But she's the one pressuring me to be more social, she's the one who's all fit and pretty and her hair doesn't frizz out and look stupid all the time, so how does she think she makes me feel? Plus, she's the one who knew I was being dumped and left out, and didn't tell me. But now I'm supposed to confide every little feeling and event to her? I'm thirteen years old! Can I not have a tiny bit of privacy without her judging me every second? I want to go to a party, is that so terrible? I'm sick of always being the bad guy here too.

Mom was making Danny some chocolate pudding, his favorite food, when it was time for me to go, and Danny was lecturing on what types of stories get put in the newspaper as if he knows anything about that, so Dad said he'd drive me. Mom didn't say anything about me wearing mascara when I said goodbye but I know she noticed, and obviously she knew she hadn't bought me any. She just went back to stirring the chocolate pudding and listening to Danny on the topic of journalism.

Dad didn't turn on the radio, so I braced myself for a Talk.

"Niki," he finally started when we were almost at Isabel's.

"What?"

"Pick you up at ten?"

"How about ten thirty?" I asked. I didn't want to seem babyish, leaving before everybody else. Ava hadn't said what time the party was ending.

"Fine. I'll be asleep by then, so it'll probably be Mom," he said. "Don't drag it out. You know she has that open house tomorrow."

"Okay." I waited. He didn't say anything else, about being true to my values or making good choices or anything, though I knew I deserved it.

He parked in front of Isabel's. I waited for it. *Come on, Dad, get to it.*

"Have fun, sweetheart," he said.

I don't know if that was some kind of psychological warfare or reverse psychology or something, but whatever. "Thanks, Dad," I said quickly. He smiled at me, without showing any teeth.

I gave him a kiss and got out of the car.

There were a lot of steps up to Isabel's house.

A bunch of adults, mostly Tobins, were sitting on the front porch, which they call the piazza. They watched me come up the steps. Most of them had drinks in plastic cups, and sweaters over their shoulders. A few had cigarettes.

"Hi, Niki," Isabel's mom called to me.

"Is that Kathryn's friend Nicole?" Isabel's ancient grandmother asked.

"No, Isabel's friend," Isabel's mom answered. "You remember Niki Ames."

"No, I don't," the grandmother said. "Ames?"

She's met me a hundred times. I said, "Hi."

She squinted at me. "Who are your parents?"

"The accountant and the real estate lady," Isabel's mom answered for me. "Suzi used-to-be-Leeds, now she's Suzi Ames. You remember her."

"No, I don't," the grandmother said. "How do you know what I remember?"

"You do. She was adorable, dated Jerome-who-died?"

"Oh, her," Grandma said. "She was adorable."

"Tell your mom I said hello," Isabel's mom told me. "Tell her she should come over and get a bazz on, sometime. I forgive her for being so young and cunning and friends with my sistah. Go around back. They're all in there making a mess."

"Thanks," I said.

As I rounded the corner to the side of the house, I heard Isabel's mom saying, "Niki's the one with the brother I told you about, from the paper."

*OMG, it was in the paper that Danny was getting tested???*

"Oh, that kid?" one of them asked. "I read that piece!"

"Shhh," Isabel's mom whispered. "Nobody wants to hear your opinion, Charles."

I wanted to, actually.

Also, I wanted to fall into a deep hole and never come back up. This is what Mom was afraid of, I guess, about having Danny tested. Of course everybody on the whole of Snug Island knew about it by now. Maybe nobody in eighth grade had read the paper.

It was in the *paper*? What is even wrong with people? We should move. Someplace big, where nobody knows us.

Boston or New York City or one of those places, where a kid getting some tests done because he's a quirky duck would not count as breaking news. Is that why Danny was talking about what's in the paper? Ugh, why didn't I listen to him? It's so hard to know when he's just randomly spewing and when it's important.

I could hear people inside before I even knocked.

Nobody answered.

If I walked to the ferry and got on, how far could I get from here before anyone found me? Or even looked for me?

I stood with my back to the door, looking down the hill toward the creek that runs behind the Tobins' house. Their cousins live two houses over, and a few other cousins live in a bunch of the other old houses all around Squall Pond and the creek.

My cousins live outside Philadelphia. Maybe we could move there.

I knocked again.

Mom hates when people ring our bell because it makes Fumble bark like crazy—great watchdog: if someone just barges right in, he runs over tail wagging, tongue lolling like the greeting committee, but if someone rings the bell? They are obviously the ENEMY and we are UNDER ATTACK.

I pushed the door open.

Isabel's huge, ancient dog, Beast, was lying on the floor in the mudroom. She lifted her head, slightly curious, as I stepped around her and the hundreds of boots and jackets and bags toward the kitchen.

Isabel's older sisters were arranging carrots around a hummus bowl, arguing about whether anybody would eat carrots when there were chips and *When will the pizza get here? How long ago did you call? I don't know! I wasn't timing myself, hands off, hands off, you gross pig! Ow, she slapped me! Grow up, wouldja, ya gawmy pissant?*

I tried to will Isabel to see me, to say hello and seem happy to see me. She was busy opening a jar of salsa and listening to Madeleine, whose voice is quiet; Isabel was bent toward her. Isabel's hair was back in a messy ponytail. I pulled my hair tie out from my half-up style and redid it as a loose ponytail. Madeleine was going on and on. It seemed like it was a funny story, whatever she was telling, because Isabel was nodding and smiling. The jar of salsa opened and both Madeleine and Isabel laughed at the burping sound it made. I smiled too, but nobody was looking at me.

I kept the smile on my face as I looked around, pretending I was perfectly comfortable, no big deal that nobody had said hello to me other than the dog. Some of Isabel's brothers have beards practically, all big and wearing flannel shirts with the sleeves rolled up. Two of them were grabbing at the chips and the carrots as they stomped through, getting swatted away by Isabel.

Her aunt came in from the piazza holding a red plastic cup and said, "Here's the party!" She opened the fridge and stood in front of it with her hands on her hips.

"Can we move Granny's coffin?" Isabel asked her.

"Can't you just work around it?"

Isabel sighed. "I guess, but it really freaks some of my friends out."

"It freaks me out," Britney announced enthusiastically, bopping into the kitchen from around the corner. "Completely!"

"Why?" asked one of the big brothers. "It's just a coffin."

"Because it's a coffin!" Britney argued.

"It's *my* coffin," Isabel's granny announced, wandering into the kitchen too, which was a relief, because I honestly was starting to think maybe she was actually dead, and I'd just hallucinated her being on the porch gossiping about my family, when actually she was lying in a coffin we were about to have a party around and not to be a baby but YIKES.

I've always felt a little immature and twitchy at Isabel's house, but it had been a while and this time, it was way worse. There was so much going on, so many people talking so fast, so much noise. And it suddenly hit me that maybe Isabel didn't know Ava had invited me, that nobody wanted me there except Ava. And where was *Ava*? Maybe she was running late, or not coming, and everybody would think I just showed up randomly. I felt like I might get run over by one of the big brothers or laughed at by everybody or even just asked, nicely, why I was there. *Please don't let that happen.* Maybe I could slip out before anybody fully registered my presence? Why did I not remember that every time I went to Isabel's house in elementary school I felt like I had to go hide in a corner, and at that point there wasn't a coffin.

*There's a coffin???*

The smaller of the two huge Isabel brothers grabbed Granny's hands and swung her around in a dance move. She smiled up at him and twirled under his arm. "Granny, we almost lost you this summer," he said.

"Nah, I'm still clingin' to the riggin'," she responded. "Oooo, chips." She grabbed a Dorito out of the bag.

"Granny, we gave you last rites," Isabel said.

"That's true," said Granny. "The priest came over, such a cute priest he is too."

Isabel's sister Kallista laughed. "Look at Granny, trying to corrupt another priest!"

"I can't help it if they find me irresistible," Granny said.

"The coffin is still right there in the living room, Granny," Kallista said. "You have to admit, it was kind of touch and go for a month there."

"Oh, just a dite, don't make a circus. Isn't it beautiful?" Granny asked. "Have you seen my coffin?" She fixed me with her pale blue eyes, almost accusing me. I was still holding my fleece. Everybody else looked at me too.

I shook my head. "Uh, no, not yet."

"Oh, hi, Niki!" Isabel said. "Rhys is here. He'll be happy to see you. Hey, Rhys!"

"She loves showing that coffin off to her friends," the taller brother said to me.

"And to *my* friends," Isabel said. "Niki, put your fleece down and come on in!"

Is it bad that I was relieved Isabel was clearly referring to me as her friend?

"It's beautiful, a beautiful coffin," Granny said, fixing me with her blue eyes. She swallowed the Dorito and grabbed a few more. "Mahogany. With the carvings. Hand carved. A beautiful cross and rosary. You have to look."

"Okay," I promised.

"Labor Day weekend, when all the cousins came from off island, there were twenty-five of us in the house," Isabel said. "We almost used the coffin as a bed that weekend."

"I was totally down," Isabel's adorable little brother Zane said, passing us on his way to the refrigerator. "I'm down for tonight, too. It's wicked soft, way sweeter than the cot I ended up on."

"Hi, Zane," I said to him. He's in Danny's grade, a cool kid, probably mean to Danny. He lifted his pointy chin in greeting back. Suddenly I was noticing chins.

"It is lovely," Granny said. "All satiny inside. I offered . . ."

"You can't sleep in your own coffin, Granny," Isabel told her.

"Whose should I sleep in?" Granny asked.

"Better Granny than somebody else sleeping in it," the bigger brother said. "With his stinky feet."

"Hey!" Zane objected. "My feet smell like roses!"

"Close the fridge, ya gawmy freak," the skinny brother told him.

"Soon I *will* sleep in it," Granny said. "For eternity. May as well get comfortable."

"Granny!" Isabel objected.

Granny shrugged. "Don't be spleeny. It's true."

"Who let these pissants in?" the biggest brother yelled from the mudroom. We turned in the direction of his voice to see Milo and Robby, and Chase.

"It's a party," Granny said, clapping her hands. "Would you boys like to see my coffin? It's beautiful."

"Um . . ." Milo said, and shot an alarmed look at me.

I nodded, eyes wide like, *Yes, an actual coffin*. He smiled.

"We're going down cellah, Granny," Isabel told her, and kissed her cheek. "Try not to die yet, okay?"

"Doing my best," Granny said.

"Good job so far," Isabel said, grabbing the chips.

Britney took the carrots and hummus. "Niki, can you get that jug of soda?"

"Sure," I said, happy to have something to do with my hands, happy to be included.

Rhys was standing near the cellar door. "Hi, Rhys," I said.

He looked at his feet.

"Hi, Rhys," Milo echoed.

"Hi," Rhys muttered to us as we passed him.

Out of the corner of my eye, I spotted the coffin, off center in the living room, diagonal to the big sagging couch.

In fairness, it did look very beautiful.

# 33

I SAT ON a big green chair. Isabel's basement has a Ping-Pong table and an air hockey, so people were playing those. Milo was playing air hockey against Robby. I had nobody to talk to. I was trying to just smile, fit in. They were all laughing and getting along and I was just sitting there, regretting everything, when Ava ran down the stairs and posed at the bottom.

"I'm here! The party can start!"

"Thank goodness!" Britney yelled, and ran over to whisper something into Ava's ear. Ava laughed and flipped her hair off her shoulder.

I was so swamped with jealousy, I could feel it radiating off me in near-visible waves. Like heat. The attention Ava was giving Britney was cooking me from the inside, for sure, but more than that, it was how relaxed and fully herself Ava looked, leaning over the banister to listen to Britney. I couldn't even feel happy for her, is how bad a best friend I am: I wanted to punch Britney, and maybe Ava, too, right in their perfect post-braces teeth, for being so easy with each other. *See me*, I thought at Ava. *Look at me like that.*

Maybe coming was a terrible idea, I was thinking. I could be cutting up catalogs with an X-Acto knife and doing something to a ramekin, whatever that is. Instead of being ignored, forced to watch my best friend look so happy with somebody else.

As I was about to try to escape out the sliding glass door, Ava yelled, "Niki!"

She dashed over and flopped into the chair with me.

"Oh," I said, making room for her in the chair, which was crammed full of me, relief, and delight.

"You're good, no worries," Ava said, and gave me a quick squeezy hug. "You came! I'm so glad!"

No words. Just appreciation. Everything was okay in the world.

Ava popped right back up, saying, "Come on!"

Kallista was bringing a stack of pizza boxes down. I followed Ava over to the Ping-Pong table, where she was telling Chase and Bradley they had to take a break from their fierce game so we could eat. I caught the ball Chase had served, just before it hit Isabel's head.

"Nice catch," Chase said.

"Thanks!" I flipped the ball at him, all casual, as if catching a ball was just a normal thing for me, not something to brag about to everybody like honestly I wanted to because *Did you see that catch, holy crow, did I catch that? Me?! MVP of Ping-Pong!*

"Saved my face," Isabel said.

"Worth saving," Bradley said.

Everybody went *awwww* and both Isabel and Bradley blushed.

"What?" Bradley said. "I just meant . . ."

"We know what you meant, doofus," Chase said, and shoved Bradley toward Isabel. He stumbled forward but didn't crash into her, and then touched her arm lightly. She looked at him.

I thought she was going to say something funny, as usual, but instead she closed her eyes and leaned toward him, and then they kissed.

Right there in front of us.

They just kissed.

Not for just a second, either. Like, they had time to put their arms around each other and still keep kissing.

Is this a thing that is happening, like, that we do? That we're supposed to do? I thought we weren't, well, up to *that*. Not to be a baby about it but WHAT? Potentially more impossible to imagine doing *that* than stealing nail polish.

I was standing an inch away, practically between them, with the heat of the pizzas in their boxes behind me and the kissers in front of me, trapped and sweating.

I didn't want to stare but I think, in hindsight? I was staring.

I felt a tug on my wrist. It was Chase, pulling me to the side. Thank goodness. Chase has the kind of laugh that sounds like a threat, and his smile seems more angry than happy, but he pulled me to the side at just the right moment, so I whispered, "Thanks."

That's when the kiss finished.

Isabel opened her eyes and turned toward the pizza boxes, like nothing had happened.

"Who's hungry?" she asked.

Everybody was. I was afraid to make eye contact with anyone because what if my eyes were boinging out of my head in shock like a cartoon character's, and everybody else was like no big deal, who *doesn't* go around kissing like that, you baby who probably still wants to jump on beds?

"Milo thought you hadn't even heard about the party," Isabel whispered to me.

"What?" I said. "Oh, I . . ."

"I told him Ava had invited you but you said you didn't like parties." She handed me a slice of pizza on a paper plate. "He seemed bummed."

"I said what? When did Ava say that?"

"Last week!" Isabel said. "Oh, I didn't take it personally, don't worry."

"No, no, the thing is I didn't . . . Last week? You said Ava told you she invited me last week and I said no?"

"I think Milo is glad you changed your mind too." Isabel winked. "Maybe you should go get some soda." She turned me by the shoulders toward the beverages.

"I didn't change . . ."

Bradley grabbed her by the hand while I was talking. She spun around toward him and they both kind of melted toward each other.

I mumbled, "Oh, okay," toward her back, and went obediently to where the drinks were. I hate soda, so I was looking for some plain water, and also something to do as an activity.

"What's your favorite soda?" Milo asked, standing up behind the bar.

"None," I admitted.

"Me either," he said. "I was looking for plain water back here."

"Same," I said.

"Also scallops," he said.

"You're looking for scallops?"

"No. I don't like soda or scallops."

"The texture," I said.

"Slimy," he agreed.

"My parents love them."

"Mine too," he said. "And okra."

"Never had it."

"Also slimy," he said. "Trust me."

"I do," I said.

He smiled a tiny bit, which made my hands all twitchy.

*OMG, how am I thirteen years old without a clue how to have a conversation?*

"But the thing I hate about soda is that it's too spicy."

"Spicy?"

"It makes my eyes cry."

"Just your eyes?" *Shut up, Niki, why are you mocking him?!*

"Yeah," he said. "Soda doesn't make me *sad*. It doesn't make me cry from my *soul*. Just from my eyes."

"Sometimes you cry from your soul?"

"Of course. Don't you?"

"I don't . . ."

"You don't cry?"

"Not lately," I lied.

"Oh," he said. He nodded and looked at his sneakers.

"Niki!" Ava called. "You are the slowest person! What are you doing?"

"Getting a . . . Be right there. Do you want soda?"

"No, I'm good!" she yelled.

"I know exactly what you mean, though," I whispered quickly to Milo. "It's just . . ."

"What?"

"Funny," I said. "Too spicy, and your eyes crying versus . . ."

Man, how dark brown are his eyes? Like, you-can't-even-see-the-pupils dark. Weird to imagine them crying. Ever. *Do eighth-grade boys cry? Does Milo cry? From his SOUL?*

"Funny like weird?" he asked.

"No," I said. "Not at all."

I went back to the green chair and squished in next to Ava. Chase sat down on the chair's arm, next to me. "You're the best wingman," Ava whispered. "I knew I could count on you."

I turned to her like, *For what?*

"We were shooting hoops before," Chase said.

Ava swallowed the pizza that was in her mouth. "Amazing," she said.

I looked from one to the other of them. *Amazing?* Okay.

Ava took another big bite. Chase shoved half his slice into his mouth. We all chewed. Chase is such a skull-head, you could see his jaw mechanism working at it.

Ava leaned close to my ear and whispered, "Pretend I'm saying something funny but also a little evil, so he thinks I'm cool."

I swallowed, opened my mouth wide, then clamped my hand over it. "Ava!" I gasped.

"What did she say?" Chase asked.

"I'll never tell," I swore, then whispered in Ava's ear, "Like that?"

She nodded, glanced at Chase, then down at her pizza.

"Like I care," Chase said.

"What?" Ava asked. "You're so funny, Chase."

"I am?"

Ava stared at her pizza. I could see she was trying not to laugh.

"I freaking love pizza," Chase said, picking some rubber off his flip-flop's sole. "I could probably eat a whole pie myself."

I had just taken a bite of my slice but Ava's little strangled laugh-noises set me off. That and how she kept staring at her pizza slice, like, *Are you a good slice? Do I want you?* I wasn't even faking; I was totally having a giggle attack from it, and from *I freaking love pizza.* But mostly from the happiness of being smooshed into a chair with Ava, laughing together, like it used to be.

Ava started choking on her pizza, laughing too. I hit her on her back and she was like, "STOP, STOP, why are you beating me up?"

I answered, "DON'T CHOKE TO DEATH, AVA!"

"I'm not!" she managed, between coughs and laughs.

"Well, good job so far, then," I said, as Isabel had said to her granny.

Ava and I opened our mouths all wide and doubled over, laughing uncontrollably again. Anytime I glanced up, Chase was just calmly chewing his pizza, which just started me dying of laughter all over again.

Then Ava leaned over and whispered to me, "Now."

"Now, what?"

"Find out if he likes me, doofus. Don't be dim."

Oh. We weren't mocking the boy Ava thought wrongly that I liked. It wasn't about me at all; it was about her. Of course. It's always about her. She liked him. Oh.

I stood up, which made the chair tip. Ava toppled toward Chase, which cracked her up that much more. I tried to laugh too, but the hilarity had passed, for me at least. So that's why she wanted me there. To be her minion. To laugh at everything she said, even if she didn't actually say anything at all, to show Chase how amazing she was. To find out for her.

To order around.

"What are you DOING, Niki?" she asked loudly enough for everybody to hear. "You're just standing there like d'oh!"

I managed to laugh a little, which made her double over, head down toward her shoes, laughing. Her backbone, above her thin T-shirt, looked like a string of beads. Really pretty. I caught Chase noticing too.

"I'm gonna, uh, go to the bathroom," I said. "I'll be, I'll talk to you, well, soon."

Ava glanced up at me and burst out laughing again, like what I'd said was the most hilarious joke any comedian had ever come up with.

I love the bathroom in Isabel's cellar. They call it the poetry bathroom. There are poems printed out and taped all over the walls, so you can just read poem after poem while you pee or poop or stall for a few minutes, away from dealing with all the people.

*Two roads diverged in a yellow wood . . .*

*The other day I was ricocheting slowly
off the blue walls of this room . . .*

*The modern biographers worry*
*"how far it went," their tender friendship.*
*They wonder just what it means . . .*

*Life is short, though I keep this from my children.*
*Life is short, and I've shortened mine*
*in a thousand delicious, ill-advised ways . . .*

As I washed my hands, dried them, and stood there holding the thin green towel, I read poem after poem, reassuring myself that Ava trusted me, wanted me there, wanted me as her best friend. I'm the one she can trust.

*You do not have to be good*
*You do not have to walk on your knees*
*for a hundred miles through the desert repenting . . .*

Chase was right outside the door as I walked out; I didn't even notice and kind of smashed into him.

"Sorry!" I quickly said. The last lines of the last poem I'd read were still echoing in my head: *Tell me, what is it you plan to do with your one wild and precious life?*

"Shhhh," Chase answered.

"Oh!" I whispered. "I have to ask you—"

"Can I, I need . . ."

"Oh, sorry, go ahead," I said, stepping to the side to let him into the bathroom. How embarrassing. How long had he been standing there waiting to use the bathroom while I feasted on poem after poem? He must've thought I was having a poop attack.

He stepped to the side, like we were dancing, instead of going into the bathroom.

"Sorry," I said. "I wasn't—I was just reading the . . ."

He was staring into my eyes. "Shhhh."

"Are you okay?" I whispered.

He pulled me by the elbow away from the main room, back toward the storage area, where the shelves full of big plastic boxes and cardboard boxes and old broken toys line the cement walls, and the, I don't know, machinery of the cellar is. Where it's dark and the rug gives up, so it's just the cold concrete floor.

"What's wrong?" I whispered.

"I have to ask you a question," Chase whispered, leaning close so his mouth touched my hair.

"Okay," I whispered back. "I have one for you, too. It would be pretty funny if it's the same question, right? Or, about the same person . . ."

"Shhh," he hushed. "You can't tell anybody. You promise?"

I nodded. I didn't want to mess up, even though, yuck, Chase Croft. How could Ava like him? But that's not fair. He's always been nice enough to me. And, people have different taste. No commenting on other people's food choices. So what if Ava likes Chase, and shoplifting, and the Squad? Why am I so judgmental?

Chase pulled back a little and looked at me. His eyes were

cold, Squall-Pond-in-early-May blue. He narrowed them, and tightened his mouth. "Niki," he whispered. "I . . ."

I nodded. He was nervous. Scared, even. That made him seem less scary and tough than usual, less like his picture should be on the outside of a bottle of poison. Some defenselessness under the tough thugishness.

"It's okay," I whispered, wondering if he had a problem, something in his family, maybe. Feeling jealous that his best friend, Bradley, has a girlfriend, or maybe he's having trouble in school, like with math. Maybe he likes Ava and feels worried she doesn't like him back. Well, he was in luck, if so! Maybe he had a sense he could trust me for exactly the reason Ava likes (or used to like) me—good listener, caring, wholesome. Not in the Squad. So he trusted me enough to confide what was troubling him.

That's what I was thinking.

Then he kissed me.

# 34

I TRIED TO push him away, but his hands were holding my arms and his mouth was clamped hard onto mine. I could feel the solid teeth behind his slightly chapped lips, and his bony body pressed against mine. I was trapped between him and the cold concrete wall. I couldn't breathe.

*My first kiss*, I was thinking, and also, *OH NO OH NO*.

I yanked my head backward, which detached me from him, at least my face.

His eyes opened.

His fingers were still tight on my arms, digging in, making tide-pool dents.

I picked up my hands and pushed back against his chest, but he didn't let go. I waved my fingers between us, to show I wasn't trying to attack him or push or make it into a *thing*. I held them up, like surrendering.

He let go of my arms.

I still could feel the imprints of his fingerprints on the flesh of my arms, and of his mouth on mine.

"Sorry," I whispered.

And I ran into the main area, away from him.

# 35

WHEN I GOT back into the main room of the cellar, Ava looked up right away, like *so?*

I shook my head microscopically, like, *Sorry, no, doesn't seem like he wants to ask you out actually.* Which felt almost like a lie, because it was so much worse than that.

No way I could just sit back down and eat more pizza and laugh. If I opened my mouth to speak, a swarm of bees might fly out.

Or, worse, sobs.

I heard Chase's footsteps approaching from behind me, from the dark place.

I turned around, opened the sliding door to the back-yard, and started throwing up before my back foot was all the way out.

I could hear everyone behind me screeching and cursing and jumping away, but there was nothing I could do beyond finish puking up all the pizza and the feeling of Chase's mouth against mine.

Like a bruise.

Like it was going to mark my lips forever in Kiss Sharpie.

No eraser would ever be able to wipe my mouth clean of it.

Ava's hand on my back. "Dude," she said.

"Ugh," I groaned.

"Could you stop?" Ava demanded, whispering so our friends inside Isabel's cellar wouldn't hear. She had one hand on my back and the other holding her nose to avoid smelling my puke, so she sounded like she had a cold.

I glanced up at her, like, as if I am doing this on purpose?

"Are you sick? Why did you come to the party if you were just gonna puke? Did you ask Chase? What did he say?"

I closed my eyes and tried to stop being distracted and think fast: what and how much to tell Ava.

The tricky part was, what if she somehow felt like I was showing off, that Chase kissed me instead of her? *Ava's fragile.*

My stomach swirled around and around. Then a weird scary thing seized up my body: it went through the motions of puking in an even bigger way than before but there was nothing left in my stomach to puke. Nothing came out, just a bit of spit.

"What, are you faking now?" Ava asked.

"No," I managed. Then I did it again, the whole, everything a body does when it's puking, except the puking bit.

"What are you *doing?*"

"I don't know, man," I said.

"Are you possessed by evil spirits or something?"

"Maybe?"

"Close the door!" Bradley yelled. "We can smell it in here."

Ava closed the door behind us.

"Niki, really, are you sick?"

She sounded worried about me. *She really is a good friend and she wanted me here because I'm the one she trusts with the secret that she likes Chase and she's vulnerable, which she hates—and now I have to tell her this? Ugh.* I closed my eyes. "I'm okay," I said.

She put her cool palm on my forehead. "You don't have a fever."

"I know it. It's not that."

I would want to know. If the roles were reversed, I would want her to tell me what the boy had done to her, right away, and then I would be hundred percent on her side, hating that boy, comforting her, yelling at him. She would never hesitate to tell me, if it had happened to her. Of course. What kind of person would hesitate to tell her best friend when something awful had happened to her? Why am I so distrustful? *You can tell me anything*, we always tell each other.

"So? What happened?" she asked.

I wiped my runny nose on the back of my hand and told myself to just tell her, just be honest. "Chase tried to kiss me," I said. "It was horrible. I came out of the bathroom and he . . ."

"You kissed Chase?"

"No," I said.

"You just said . . ."

"He kissed me."

"Uhh, kissing is a mutual . . ."

"Yeah, it's supposed to be," I said. "That's what I'm . . ."

"You knew I liked him. But you . . ."

"I nothing!" I took a deep breath and tried to settle both my stomach and my voice. "This is what—listen. I came out of the bathroom and . . ."

"And he just kissed you, without saying anything?" Her hands were on her hips, her pink lips tucked in, a tight line across her angry face. Doubting me.

"No," I said.

"No?"

"He said . . ." I tried to think. "He said he had a question, and I figured it was about you, so I was like, okay."

"You said okay."

"I said . . ." *She's jealous*, I reminded myself. *She seems so strong, but I am the only one who knows she's actually fragile.*

"Ava," I started again. "It was nothing, I just, I'm overreacting . . ."

"He went to kiss you and you said okay."

"Oh, Ava, no, that's not what . . ."

"So you were lying? You just said you said okay."

"I don't remember exactly what I said! I wasn't recording it."

"You don't have to get snotty," Ava said.

"I didn't—sorry," I said. "Sorry. That's mostly what I said, actually. Sorry."

"'Sorry'? You said 'Sorry'?"

"Yes! He kissed me hard, like a punch, and I was like, Sorry! Isn't that so dumb?"

"Why would you say sorry if you hadn't done anything wrong?"

"I know it, right?" I sniffed. The pukey smell was gross but it was mixed with the strong scent of honeysuckle from the yard and the salty cool air coming up from the creek. I tried to focus my smelling on the honeysuckle and the salt.

"No," Ava said. "I mean, it doesn't make sense. You must have known you'd done something wrong, if you were apologizing."

I shook my head. "It's a bad habit of mine."

"Or you knew you'd been flirting with him, doubling over laughing so hard, flicking your hair around. God, I'm so dumb. I thought you hated him."

"I do," I said. "I mean, I don't *hate* him, if you like him, I just . . ."

"I thought you were helping *me* flirt with him."

"I was!" My whole body was suddenly freezing cold, shivering. *She's sad and needs my support. That's all this is. A test. I'm usually good at tests. FOCUS.* "Ava, you know I was helping you flirt, not that you needed anybody's—I mean, not that you were overdoing it, at all! Just that, I mean, you're the cutest girl in the whole . . ."

"I am not."

"You are. And the most fun, the funniest, if he doesn't see how amazing you are, he's just dumber than a pounded thumb!"

"You think he's dumb."

"No, Ava, no. I'm just saying anything now to make you . . . I'm just . . ." *Ugh, I sounded just like my mother, soprano and rambling, pleading, desperate. BE REAL. BE CLAM.*

"I thought you were my best friend," Ava said.

"I am," I said. *Everything I am saying and NOT saying right now is because I am your best friend!* I screamed. But only inside my head. The words that came out were just, "Ava, come on, you know I am. . . ."

"I can't believe you," she said. "This whole time I thought you're too wholesome and pure and babyish for me. But that wasn't the problem at all. I can't believe I didn't realize what a fake friend you've been, this whole time."

"Fake?"

"You hate him, you don't hate him, you kissed him, you didn't kiss him. You're just saying anything. . . . Did you just use me to get with Chase?"

"Hundred percent no," I said. "Ava. I think I like Milo. *Like him*, like him."

"Well, you suck at flirting, in that case, if you're making out with the boy I like instead. Everybody warned me, but I was like, No, you don't know Niki like I do."

"Wait, what?" I asked, wrapping my arms around myself. "What did everybody say?"

"Of course, *that's* what you care about," Ava said.

"I don't! Ava, I'm telling you what happened, and I'm really shook, and I need . . ."

"*You* need," Ava said. "And that's all that matters. The world has to revolve around whatever you want? Why don't you call your mom?"

"Call my *mom*?"

"She's the one who taught you that the only thing that matters is what *you* want, right? That's how your whole family acts. But the problem with that is, you and Danny—this is exactly what everybody says, if you really want to know the truth. This, exactly. You have to be the center of everything. You need *all* the attention."

"I so don't," I said. "And Danny? Danny isn't the center of anything, so—I don't even know what you're—what?"

Ava shook her head. "It's just a coincidence that as soon as I mention I might like somebody, you're the one kissing him? How is that friendship? And you can't even just try to steal him from me, you have to make it more drama, like, what, like he 'sexually assaulted' you? Should we call the police because a boy kissed you, is that what you want? So now you can be such a victim and be famous on the news, like you always say you want to be? Don't lie, you know I know everything about you. That's what you want, you always say it. You want to be famous, and on the TV, like my mom was. But this is just *sad*, Niki."

"Ava, no . . ."

"Why are you so desperate for everyone's attention right now, is my question. Is it because of your big exaggeration about going blind like Laura frigging Ingalls and poor you, your brother is a freaking weirdo the whole town is talking about because the garbage men came to his birthday party and it was in the newspaper?"

"It was?" *Don't say actually it was Mary not Laura who went blind in the Little House on the Prairie books, don't be that person.* "Wait—what was in the paper about Danny?"

"Like you didn't know about the story of his tearjerker birthday party. Your name was on the photo credit. Come on, Niki, don't play innocent. But even all that didn't get you enough attention today? How much more do you need?"

I shook my head. "Ava, I swear I don't . . ."

"I know you're having a crappy childhood because all the attention is focused on your brother, but . . ."

"What? I'm not having a crappy . . ."

"Of course you are, and everybody feels sorry for you about it. But, come *on*. Boo freaking hoo. Everybody knows all the attention in your family is focused on your brother's issues and that's why your mom lashes out at everyone and ignores you. We all feel bad for you about it, and for having a brother like that. But you're like an addict. Enough."

I just stood there blinking at her. I wasn't even insulted for myself anymore but for Danny, and my parents, and, well, okay, also for myself. A little. Maybe. Crappy childhood? No, the thing about me is the opposite of that; I have to check my privilege because I have it the easy way, everything is easy and good for me WHAT?!?!

I was so confused.

I wasn't hurt, or sad, or sorry for her anymore. I didn't even know what I was feeling. Cold. Just cold.

*For having a brother like that?*

"Danny is great," I said.

"Yeah, sure," Ava said quietly. "I tried. I tried helping you hang out with the popular kids. But honestly, Niki, now I'm just *done*."

She stepped carefully over my pile o' puke and smiled big, dimples deep, as she opened the sliding door. She stepped through and closed it behind her.

I realized there were tears streaming down my cheeks, even though I honestly just felt empty, not upset. But with tears falling down and puke on my boots, there was no way I could go back inside. *You can't go back.* It was dark, or nearly dark, out there, so I could stand halfway behind the bush and see nobody was looking for me.

A burst of laughter from inside hit me like a brutal wave, knocking me over, sand in my mouth and feet kicking my own head.

I walked around the side of the house.

There were still adults on the front porch, gossiping.

I pressed my back up against the house like I was in a spy movie, not wanting the adults to spot me. Maybe also slightly, a tiny bit, wondering if anybody would come to look for me. I didn't want to get too far away, in that case.

No footsteps, no door sliding open.

Maybe soon, give it a minute.

The only noises were night noises, the thrum of the waves

way down the hill at the beach, and the murmuring voices of Isabel's old people on the porch. No kids. Nobody calling my name.

A billion stars in the sky.

I stood there and looked at them.

*Is anybody else looking at this sky right now, feeling alone in the universe too? Are you out there, my someone? If I wish on a star, and you wish at the same exact second, will we find each other someday and feel less alone? Will you find me? Choose me? Who are you, you who will choose me, know me, see me, believe me? Be a pair with me?*

So many stars.

Each burning bright.

Each alone. Hang on. Maybe not alone. Maybe . . . independent.

And together, lighting the universe.

While underneath them, I tried to keep myself anchored to the fragile blue marble spinning ceaselessly through the silent sky, or however Dad said it.

Perspective?

Okay. My perspective? Nobody was coming after me. If I told Ava what I was thinking about while looking at the stars, she'd just say I was being a drama queen space cadet fake poetic nerd.

I texted my mom: **not feeling great—can you come pick me up? I'll be at the corner down the hill from Isabel's.**

I put my phone in my pocket and cut through the neighbor's yard.

What if Danny's having a tantrum and Mom's phone is in

the other room? We live pretty far from Isabel's, in the newer section, nearer to town. I guess I could walk home.

My phone buzzed in my pocket. I made a wish for it to be Ava.

Opened my eyes to see. Nope. Mom: **You okay?**

I stared at that for a minute.

**No**, I typed and deleted.

**Fine just**

**I threw up so I**

**I was on my way out of the bathroom and Chase**

Delete delete delete

**Niki?** Mom texted after I gave up trying to text an answer to her unanswerable question.

But then I thought of the right answer:

**Do I have to?**

I stood in the starlight, on the slope of Isabel's neighbor's backyard, praying, *Please remember our old code.*

Three pulsing dots on my phone's screen.

**Be right there**, Mom texted.

**Thanks**, I texted back.

I walked down the hill, with my arms wrapped around me. The night wasn't so cold, but still I was a little chilled. My fleece. Oops. Left it at Isabel's, upstairs in the mudroom.

Oh well. Not going back. Dad would be mad. He hates when we lose our stuff. Though he didn't notice my sneakers had been missing. Maybe nobody would even notice if bits of me are scattered and missing.

Am I invisible?

Do I even exist, or am I imagining myself?

I got to the bottom of the hill and sat down on the curb to wait.

I closed my eyes and inhaled the night smells, the honey-suckle and the salt from the ocean down at the beach. I considered crying but that felt so extra, I didn't. Couldn't. It wouldn't be just crying from my eyes, and I might never stop.

Instead I sang myself the Okay Song.

I was still sitting on the curb with my eyes closed, singing *Okay, okay* quietly to myself, when I heard the tires approaching.

I hadn't gotten up to the silence yet.

# 36

"I DON'T KNOW," I told her. "Maybe I'm allergic to soda."

"You drank soda?"

"Yeah."

"I thought you hated soda."

"I do."

I didn't drink soda. Not sure why I didn't tell her what had actually happened. She is so good to talk things through with. Especially when it's just the two of us, especially in the car. She's a really good listener and completely, automatically, hundred percent on my side.

But she was already talking about Danny and what he was doing tonight, and that he had come right when she called him, without any argument! Like it was a huge accomplishment. And, like, great.

But also, I can't care about that right now, Mom, sorry.

Sorry, sorry, sorry.

My phone in my lap, cold and silent as the night, the whole way home.

Beside me while I washed the makeup off my face.

Next to my pillow.

Next to my bruised mouth that hadn't yelled NO or I DON'T WANT YOU at him.

That hadn't said I NEED TO YOU TO CARE ABOUT ME, AVA.

My mouth that was only full of *sorry*.

# 37

I WAS SITTING with the clipboard, rearranging the postcards and information sheets on the granite countertop while Mom showed a tourist couple around. They had the summer-people uniforms: matching boat shoes, toothy smiles, sun-blasted faces. I was trying to imagine them living in the house, him waking up early to clean their sleek sailboat, her loping down the hill a little later, holding steaming mugs of coffee for before they set sail. Maybe they'd have a dog, a golden Lab. Some golden kids to match.

I'd offered them their choice of still or sparkling water. The woman chose sparkling. The man said he'd share hers. She said, "Fat chance." He laughed.

I liked them. Good prospects. I could hear Mom's voice but not her words as she led them up the front stairway. Like wind chimes, happy and relaxed.

Maybe they'll buy it, and Mom will be happy, and make a

bunch of money, to pay for whatever Danny ends up needing.

*Please let them buy it for the asking price,* I prayed.

*Please let there be something Danny needs that money can buy. I will chip in all the money I make in my life to pay for it, I swear to all the gods I will fully believe in if they make my brother fixable.*

The door opened and a family walked in, so I smiled and said hi. They looked vaguely familiar even all the way over at the door, all blurry, but I figured maybe they were summer people I'd seen at Scoops or at the beach in August. "Welcome!"

When they got to the kitchen, I saw the kid behind them was Milo. Both of his parents were tall and slim, but the mom had darker skin and shiny black hair like Milo. There was something quiet about both of the parents, just like Milo: a sort of comfort in their own skin, not having to blurt or perform or smile all big like the tourists exclaiming about the view upstairs with Mom. Like so many people.

"Oh, hi," I said to Milo, too loud maybe.

"Hey, Niki," he said. "You okay?"

"Yeah, I, oh, yeah. I didn't realize it was you guys! I forgot my glasses at home, so you're blurry again! But I'm fine! How are you?"

They all just blinked at me and nodded.

Too much. Great.

I pushed the clipboard toward his mom and didn't tell her what to do. Instead I breathed through my nose. I didn't definitely feel the pukes coming back, but honestly, what was going on with me? One more sudden barforama and I would obviously have to run away from home to Canada and never come back.

"Thanks," his mom said, and signed in.

She and Milo's dad were already looking around. Mom had done an amazing job staging the place. That's what she calls her transformations: staging. The whole house was clean and tidy, all shiny surfaces in the kitchen, a crumble baking on low temperature in the oven. The special navy throw pillows from our couch at home perked up the couch in the family room that overlooked the ocean, just three wide steps down from the spacious kitchen. Mom had removed the heavy curtains the current owners had hung everywhere, and let the sunlight in. It's one of her major tricks, taking down the curtains, cleaning the windows. That and the crumble. And the mums dotting the garden.

Mom knows how to make things look better than they are.

"Oh, Michael, look at that view, can you imagine?" Milo's mom asked his dad.

The dad jammed his hands into his pockets and followed his wife down the steps, to imagine.

"Where's Robby?" I asked.

"Watching football. Did you have food poisoning?" Milo asked me quietly.

I shrugged. "Honestly, who knows, let's not talk about it, gross."

"Or Chase poisoning?"

"What." My fingers went icy.

"Isabel said food poisoning, but I thought . . . Chase."

"What did he say?"

"Nothing," Milo said. "A hunch."

"A hunch."

"Well, from how he was acting, and then how Ava was all nasty to him."

"She was?"

"I thought she was into him, honestly, before that, and then, well . . . so . . . ."

"She, what did she do, after I left?"

"Nothing, she was just, you know," he said.

"Sure," I lied.

I didn't want to seem like I was trying to flirt with him. Not that I know how to flirt. Or how not to. Maybe I had been flirting without meaning to with Chase, which made him punch-kiss me. *Don't think about that.*

"So," I wittily said, waving my hand like *anyway*, but with way bigger of a movement than I'd intended, so I jammed my pinky into the counter really hard. And just kept on going. The rest of my hand plus the bashed pinky bumped into the brochures and business cards, knocking some of them onto the floor. I hopped off the stool to pick them up and realized my whole body was shivering.

*Seriously, body: calm the heck down.*

Milo crouched next to me and picked some of the cards up

too. He handed me his pile. They bumped into my battered pinky. "Ouch," I said.

"Sorry!" he said. "Did I hurt you?"

"No, I just, the counter just attacked me. You saw it, right?"

"Yes," he said, all serious. He turned and faced the counter. "You stupid idiot. How dare you."

I laughed. "Thanks."

He shrugged. "Wish I'd said that to Chase, last night."

No words. What does a normal human do with her eyes?

"So, you don't have the flu, at least," Milo said after a thousand years of me dying in front of him.

"No," I managed.

"Well, that's good."

"Thanks."

*Ugh, thanks? That's what I said? Thanks?*

He nodded.

"Do you want water?" I asked. "The only other choice is club soda."

"I'm good," he said.

"Yeah," I agreed. *Somebody shoot me.* "Is your family thinking of moving?" I asked, to lighten it up.

He shrugged. "My whole life."

"Really?"

"They bought our house as a starter house."

"But haven't you lived here for . . ."

"Yeah, they bought it before we were born," he said. "But

they only planned to live in it for two years, tops. So they keep looking."

"Do you think they'll do it, someday, or do they just like looking?" I asked.

"As a hobby?"

"Lots of people do that, just enjoy looking at houses," I said. "Trust me."

"I do," he said, and smiled.

I clutched the counter with my bruised hand just as something fell upstairs. We both looked up, as if we could see what, through the ceiling. We couldn't.

"I always think they will," Milo said quietly.

"Will what?"

"I always think, anytime I'm going home alone, without Robby: I wonder if we still live there. What if I get home and they've already moved?"

"Always?"

"Every single time I ever go home alone."

"That's intense."

"Yah," he said. "Welcome to my life."

"It takes time," I said. "There's a whole process with the bank."

"I have a dream sometimes that I get home and they're gone and they forgot to take me. Or tell me."

"Yikes."

He shrugged. "They like to travel light."

I started to laugh, because Milo said it like that was funny, and with a smile, but he also looked sad at the same time. In his eyes.

"Plus they have another one just like me."

"Not *just* like."

"Pretty close," he said. "Not that many people can tell us apart."

"I can," I said, even though I sometimes can't.

"Yeah," Milo said. "Because you've lived next door all this time, I guess."

"Not just that," I said. "You're not the same."

"I appreciate that."

"Families," I said.

"Yeah," he said. "So much."

After a second, we turned toward the window. His parents were standing in front of it, their arms around each other, both looking out at the churning sea.

# 38

MOM WAS HAPPY with the way the day went, and appreciated my help. On the drive home, with all our throw pillows stacked neatly in the back seat, her phone buzzed. I picked it up. "Samantha," I said.

Mom frowned. "Shut it off," she said. "I can't deal with her today."

"What's going on?" I asked.

Mom did a loud inhale. "I just have enough—she has a lot of opinions, and, hey, here's a new rule for our family: You're not allowed to let anyone hurt you. Including yourself. Okay?"

I slumped down in my seat. "Okay," I said, then mumbled, "I'll try."

"She thinks I should put Danny in private school, a special school for kids on the spectrum."

I let that sink in. A special school? Is there even one of those on Snug Island? "What do you think?"

"I think . . ." She paused. "I don't know what I think.

I'm angry. And confused. I don't trust my instincts anymore because, honestly, what I want is everything to just be okay."

"Mmmm-hmm," I said.

"And it's my job to make everything okay if it's not, so . . ."

"No, it's not," I said. "Sometimes it's not a tie. Maybe that's okay, though."

She didn't answer, just drove.

"Or not," I said.

"No, you're right," Mom said. "We don't have a full diagnosis for Danny yet, but it looks like he's just wired a little differently. It's not a thing that needs fixing, or curing, and it's nothing to be ashamed of—he is who he is and he's just right. Maybe we can make some things easier for him, better for him, with insights from the testing, right?"

"Like how?"

"Maybe he'll get some extra help, or need some medication. He probably could benefit from therapy and coaching, to help him be his best self. Maybe a different kind of school, down the road. We'll see. There are probably things we can modify at home, too, for him. Like having schedules written down, preparing him for changes, being more organized."

"You're very organized, Mom," I said. "Seriously, you're scary good at—"

"Well." Her lower jaw jutted out over her front teeth. "Apparently there are people who think I'm not good enough." Deep breath. "It might just take me a little time to not feel like punching everybody, to protect him."

"Including me?"

"No, not you," she said, turning left into our driveway and putting the car in park. "You're the finest kind, Niki."

"No, I'm not."

"Trust me on this, you deeply are."

"Mom! Why do you always . . . You think we're perfect, and you think that helps us or something—but you don't get how invisible and failed that makes me feel, when you keep saying I'm the finest kind, because then I can't even tell you what is actually happening with me!"

"Why can't you—"

"Because you'll be disappointed in me," I said. "I want to stay the finest kind in your imagination, which is the one place I am, because in reality I'm getting kissed in cellar corners by a boy I don't like and I have nobody to talk about it with!"

"Niki, what—"

"I don't want to talk about it!"

"Okay," Mom said, touching my hand, which I yanked away.

"I will someday but not right now. Okay?"

"Okay," Mom said. "I'm here whenever you want to t—"

"I'm sorry."

"It's okay. I just want you to talk to me, tell me whatever—"

"I will. I will. I promise. I'm sorry. But . . . I'm sorry, Mom. I don't want to hurt your feelings. But you just have to stop staging our family. We have crappy curb appeal? Fine! That's us, then! Maybe nobody will want us. Too bad, you got a clunker of a family. I just can't care about that right now."

"Niki, I never for one second feel—"

"Sorry." I got out of the car and went into the house.

In my room with the door closed, I felt guilty and dumb. She was just trying to compliment me. She was sitting outside in the car with her eyes closed.

I sat on the floor against my door and checked the weather on all the different weather apps on my phone. The storm was churning up the coast, picking up steam, wrecking beaches in New Jersey. I went down a rabbit hole of nerdy weather science, to keep from thinking about my storm-tossed life, and read again that story I liked about how if the winds way high up in the atmosphere are too strong, they can shear apart a developing storm, keep it from turning into a hurricane.

Strong winds would tamp down the storm.

You need calm winds to brew a hurricane.

BE CLAM? You'll just bring on the storm.

I closed the weather apps. Went to texts. Nothing new from Ava.

Screw clam winds, then.

I texted her:

**Hey. I'm sorry I ended up kissing the boy you like. I should have been stronger and clearer with him, to make him stop.**

Sent that, but there was more. I wasn't done. So I added:

**You were really the opposite of helpful to me, after. I was**

**hurt and confused and literally puking. And you**

Send. Oops. Not done.

**And you weren't there for me. At all, Ava. You just left me all alone and you haven't even checked to see if I got home okay last night.**

Send.

**I did, btw. I'm not fragile. But I am hurt.**

I deleted that last one, turned off my phone, and got into bed.

I don't know when I fell asleep, but I woke up in the pitch dark from a nightmare, the one I used to have when I was little:

We're in the car. Me, Danny, Mom. Me and Danny both in the back seat, because it's not fair if one of us gets the front, our old rule. Mom stops the car, in the parking lot of the grocery store. She has to run in and grab a few things; we should wait in the car. She closes the door and disappears into the store, and the car starts moving. We'll crash if I can't stop the car. I jump into the front seat but can't reach the pedals, so I just steer. We're picking up speed; I'm narrowly avoiding hitting trees, other cars, a kid on a tricycle. We're on Victory Boulevard now. Zooming down the hill. I yell to Danny to help me, come into the front, get down in the well under my feet and try to find the brake. He has a million questions, he's slow unbuckling his seat belt, says he shouldn't unbuckle his seat belt when the car is moving, therefore he can't come up front, stop yelling at him, he hates being yelled at.

Puts his fingers in his sensitive ears and grunts.

I'm up on my knees, then, leaning forward, knowing it's up to me to save us.

The car is out of control and nobody can stop it, including me. I just have to keep trying to steer.

When I woke up, I was sweating, shaking.

*It was just a dream,* I told myself.

But my pounding heart didn't believe me.

# 39

EARLY IN THE morning, before everyone else was even downstairs, I got my bike out and started riding. I rode so fast, all my tears streamed back from my eyes instead of ever reaching my jawline. Just streaked back behind me like an invisible banner of salty drops. Whatever. I had cried enough from my soul already.

I wanted to leave before Mom could try to have a talk with me, or Milo and Robby were out their door. I needed to get to school before anyone so I could be ready instead of sweaty.

I was sitting in front of Holly's locker when she showed up.

"Fisherman's Friend?" she offered.

"Holly," I said.

She held out her pack of lozenges to me. I didn't take one.

"I'm not a fisherman, or anybody's friend."

She just waited while I stood up.

"I want to tell you the truth, okay?"

"Sure."

I'd been practicing it in my head since I woke up from the bad dream, saying this to her, but the rehearsal didn't make it easier. It felt like doing trust falls, like falling backward into the void, even though I was facing her this time, and the last thing I deserved was to be caught.

"I didn't get sick, and nothing bad was happening with Danny. I was happy to let you blame him, or think I was a shallow jerk for being embarrassed that maybe he'd be freaking out or whatever, but that's not why I canceled on you. It's because I got invited to a party at Isabel's."

Her hand, holding the Fisherman's Friends, slowly lowered. She didn't say anything.

"Ava invited me."

"Ayuh," Holly said.

"That's why I disinvited you. It was horrible. Which I deserved. But anyway, I thought you should know and not keep trying with me, because I actually do suck. I'm a bad friend."

I slammed my locker shut and went to first period alone.

When I got there, I put my glasses in their case in my backpack's front pocket. Nothing to see, folks. I heard Ava talking next to me, to Britney and Isabel and Madeleine, but I ignored them. This is what it means to be alone, off the ark? So be it. Come on, storm, hit me.

I avoided Holly until art class. I collected my empty elephant bowl. The crack had spread. When I put the thing down, a triangular section of it broke off, basically the whole face and trunk. Awesome. Though, tbfair, not so much worse.

I just sat in my seat, looking at it.

Ms. Hirsch walked over. "Oh, I was afraid of that. I saw the crack when I took it out of the kiln."

I held in my apology and nodded instead.

"Holly, do you remember Kintsugi method, from last year's after-school class?"

"I do," Holly said.

"Would you help Niki put her pinch pot together with that?"

"Sure," Holly said.

Ms. Hirsch bustled off to gather some supplies.

"You don't have to," I whispered. "I can just throw this whole mess out."

"It's okay," Holly said. "It's fixable." She picked up the broken triangle with her delicate fingers and fit it into the space where it had been. "In Kintsugi," she said, without looking into my eyes the way she usually did, "the artist holds the broken pieces in her hands, and really looks at the break, the crack, and sees it. Notices it. Doesn't judge it."

She handed me my wrecked pieces of garbage.

"*See it gently*," Holly whispered.

"I don't . . ." I felt as broken as the ruined bowl in my hands.

"See gently the beauty in the brokenness. Honor the art in what's broken."

I looked at her. If Ava had heard her say that, say, *See gently the beauty in the brokenness*, she'd mock her for the rest of the year. I arched an eyebrow at Holly, but Holly wasn't joking.

"Okay. And then I can throw it away?" I asked. "Now that I *honored* it? Is that the, like, thing of it? Kashonee?"

"Kintsugi," Holly said. "No. Then the artist puts the cup or the bowl or the vase back together. She doesn't try to hide the cracks. Instead she fills them with bright gold or platinum glue, or resin, I think? Sticky stuff that binds the pieces together. That's what the art is, what makes her an artist. Well, the seeing, too. But . . ."

Ms. Hirsch brought over supplies, including blue latex gloves like the ones Rhys wore in the ice cream store. We put them on, and Holly helped me glue my bowl back together, stirring gold goo into the stuff called epoxy, layering it into the cracks with the flat wooden stirrers. We worked there in silence, side by side, on my broken bowl, until the bell rang. Around us everybody else hustled out. We took off our gloves and tossed them after we cleaned up. Ms. Hirsch turned my bowl around and around in her hands, admiring it and complimenting us.

"Yeah. My scar-faced, misshapen elephant," I said. "Aren't you pretty?"

"No," Holly said. "Not pretty. But beautiful. Can't you see that?"

I looked at it, empty and lumpy and scarred. The gold was cool, I'll say that.

We went back to our table and got our stuff.

"Thanks," I said. "For helping me with that. It would be humiliating to fail eighth-grade art."

"I knew you were going to Isabel's party," Holly said, walking away. "I'm not stupid."

I watched her until she reached the door, then turned around to put my alone-in-the-world, kicked-off-the-ark elephant on a low shelf.

"Niki."

I turned around, surprised she was still there, surprised to hear my name in her voice again. "Yeah?"

"Are you coming to the library? You can tell me why the party sucked, and I'll let you tell me everything before I even gloat and tell you how much more fun you would've had if we'd done the sleepover instead."

"Holly, I so wish . . ."

"Damn straight," Holly said. "Now you'll always be one fun night down in your life because you chose to chase the nasties instead of hanging with awesome me. Hurry up."

I thought my face had permanently forgotten how to smile but apparently not.

I walked in silence with her to the library, where I told her the whole story.

She listened to every bit.

"You can gloat now," I said, when I finished.

"Chase Croft is a horse's patoot," she said.

I cracked up. "A what?"

"That's what my nana says about people like him," Holly whispered.

"So, here's the thing, though," I said. "What should I have done differently? I keep thinking about Danny, what got him in trouble? It was, well, he threw a book. At Ms. Broderick."

"Oh no!" Holly laughed. "I love Ms. Broderick. But she probably deserved it, if Danny . . ."

"No, she fully didn't," I said. "Danny was just mad because he got paired up with Margot Hu, and he didn't want her."

"Really?" Holly said. "She seems sweet. No?"

"To me, too. But Danny screamed *I DON'T WANT YOU* right in her face."

"Why?"

I shrugged. "He didn't want her? Anyway, the point is, when Chase, you know, grabbed me? I said *sorry*."

"And you should've said, *I DON'T WANT YOU!*"

"I mean, obviously not, but . . ."

Holly nodded. "You could learn some stuff from Danny."

"So true," I said.

"I'm gonna gloat now, or not gloat but just say one thing."

"Okay," I said.

"Only this: Don't dump me for Ava again. I know you love her, but she's actually very crappy to you. No offense, but there it is."

I smiled. "There it is."

The bell rang.

"I kind of deserve it, though," I said. "How crappy she is to me. I'm a bad fr—"

"NO!" Holly said. "No, you aren't perfect, obviously, but you're not bad except to yourself. Which you are stopping as of this minute. Don't be a stupid idiot. Come on."

We went to fifth period, where we had a sub who showed us videos of hurricanes to prepare us for what was about to hit us.

But the weather was the least of it, for me.

# 40

"DO YOU LIKE Chase?" Britney asked me on our way to English. She smelled like bubble gum as she steered me with her hand on my arm.

"No," I answered. "Not at all."

"He says you guys made out at the party," Britney said. "Why would you make out with him if you don't even like him? Ava says you like both him and Milo, and you're trying to seem cool, to us, or something, by acting slutty?"

"I'm hundred percent not," I said.

"You can admit it to me, if you like somebody," Britney whispered. "I'm really good at this kind of thing. I can help if you want to ask one of them out or whatever. But if you were just trying to act cool? You shouldn't disrespect yourself like that."

"Thanks," I said. "But that is not even close to what happened."

"So what happened? You just, like, made out with him randomly?" Britney asked. "Just really into making out with people? You never really seemed like that, before."

"He grabbed me and kissed me. I pushed him away."

Britney stopped, her big eyes wide open. "Wait. No. Is that the truth?"

"Hundred percent," I said.

"She told me the whole story," Holly said, behind me. "If Chase is saying something different, he's lying."

"I'm telling the truth, Britney," I said. "It was horrible. He grabbed me, kissed me, and wouldn't stop when I was pushing him away. That's why I threw up."

"That. Is horrible," Britney said. "Why didn't you say anything?"

"I don't know," I said. "I just wanted to get away, to safety, you know? And, to, like, erase it, make it never have happened."

"Niki." Britney reached out her green-nail-polished hand and touched my arm. "That's awful. You poor thing. Are you okay?"

"Yeah," I said. "I'm okay. Thank you."

"Hang on. So why did Ava say—"

I shrugged. "I don't know."

Britney blew a bubble. It popped. She sucked it back into her mouth and chewed a couple of times, thoughtfully. I wasn't sure what to do. I'm pretty conflict averse, and Britney, for all her adorableness, is fierce and fast. Her jaw was working hard on the gum chewing, and her arms were crossed, but her normally merry eyes were cool, scanning my face.

The sky outside the window in the atrium was darkening, as if night had decided to come in a hurry, like Britney's suddenly dark mood.

She turned around and started sprinting in the other direction, back toward the lockers.

"Oh . . . kay," I said to Holly. "Guess she was finished discussing that."

"That was interesting," Holly agreed.

Down the hall, Britney stopped, having caught Isabel by the arm. She made Isabel lean down toward her, and whispered something into her ear. They both swiveled their heads toward us. Holly and I still hadn't glanced at each other but we were standing shoulder to shoulder in the atrium, watching the Squad assemble.

Madeleine danced up between Isabel and Britney, who whispered to her, and now the three of them whispered, then looked at us again.

"Did we just doom ourselves?" I whispered to Holly. "Why does this feel like we're about to have a battle?"

"With those doorknobs?" she asked. "Who cares what they think? Let's go."

I smiled. If only it were that easy, to not care what they think. What magical world would you have to live in, to think it didn't matter what the Squad thinks of you? To think it wouldn't affect your day every day for the rest of eighth grade and high school?

"Yeah," I tried. "Those doorknobs."

We were just turning away, to continue on to English, when Ava reached the Squad. "Hey!" I heard her say. "I just saw Milo and Robby, and you would not—"

I don't think they answered her. Madeleine, Isabel, and Britney turned and walked away from Ava, toward us.

Holly and I stopped. Were they coming to fight us? Should I pull my hair back in a ponytail or something? I'd never gotten in a fight, a real fight, but I've seen girls do that in videos. I braced myself. Lightning lit the hallway through all the windows, right on cue.

Madeleine, Isabel, and Britney walked with their long strides right between me and Holly. As they passed us, thunder boomed, but I heard Isabel's voice perfectly well, under it.

"We believe you," Isabel said to me as they passed. Her hand squeezed my arm.

Nothing much happened in English. We were all kind of subdued and quiet, while the sky went from dark to a strangely bright greenish and the rain started lashing the windows. Ms. Carozi was going on and on about how to write a five-paragraph essay, but I was listening more to the rain than her words, and feeling the electricity in the air that I suspected was from more than just the lightning.

None of us were chatting or making faces at one another.

When the bell rang, we all got up silently and filed out.

The wind had started to really howl by the time I was trying to get my stuff out of my locker. I was dreading the bike ride home, wondering if it would be okay to just leave my bike and walk instead. I swung my backpack over my shoulder, still contemplating that, when I saw Chase, there, looming over me. My stomach clenched and I smooshed my left leg and hip practically into my locker, holding tight to the locker door that I pulled a bit more shut, between us.

"Yo," Chase said.

*Leave me alone,* I thought. *I don't want you, I DON'T WANT YOU.*

"Sorry," he mumbled.

"What?" I managed.

"Sorry," he said. "If you're upset, or . . ."

"No," I said.

"Huh?"

"Uh-uh." My hands were clenching the straps of my back-pack and I was scared, but come on. I was feeling that weird empty feeling again, like I'd felt when Ava dissed my whole family, only this time I knew the name of it. Not emptiness. Rage.

"What's 'uh-uh'?" Chase imitated.

"That's not an apology."

"If you want an engraved—"

"If you're sorry, be sorry," I said, surprising myself. A tiny voice in my head was urging me to shut up, be cool, shrug it off—but a louder voice was yelling NO, and that's the one I decided to listen to for once. I don't know. That non-apology apology just boiled me right up. "Own it. Say it. Are you sorry?"

"I just said it. Sorry if you're upset," Chase mumbled. "Ugh."

"No," I said. "You know you grabbed me, you know you kissed me and kept kissing me when I was trying to push you away, you know you did a wrong thing. Be sorry for what you did. Not *if* I'm upset. I am upset! You know I am—I'm more than upset. I threw up! You know that. You were the one person there who knew why I was puking. You knew exactly why I left. And you knew it was because of what YOU did. To me. But did you care? No. You kissed me because you wanted to, without even a thought of what I wanted."

"How am I supposed to know what you want?" Chase grunted.

*Body language*, I thought, but what I said was, "You could ASK!"

"Ask?"

"Yeah! And then listen to the ANSWER! You don't have to guess!"

"I thought you wanted to. You were, like, you seemed . . ."

"I was pushing you away," I said.

"Yeah, but . . ."

"You held on to my arms while I was pushing you away."

"Look, I said I'm sorry, okay?"

"You said you're sorry *if* I'm upset! Well, I am upset! But that is not enough of an apology."

I looked around. Everybody was staring at me. Chase's skull-face was bright red.

"Okay," he mumbled. "Sorry. Okay?"

I waited. I had never made a scene at school before. Now what?

"And you promise never to touch me again."

"Yeah," he said.

"And from now on, if you want to kiss somebody—ask first!"

"I thought you liked me," he mumbled, suddenly bashful. "I like you. So I . . ."

"You should still ask," I said, quieter. "It's super romantic, and if the person likes you back, it'll be great, I promise you. But if she doesn't, it won't be a disaster. You can accept it and be friends. But you *both* get to choose, you know?"

He nodded without lifting his eyes. "Okay. We okay?"

"I guess so," I said.

He turned around and dashed toward the stairwell. He's really fast.

Holly smiled at me. "That was awesome. You good?"

"Yeah, really good," I said. "Not pukey at all! Wanna come over?"

"Ayuh," Holly said.

# 41

ON OUR WAY out, Ava came dashing over to me. "Hey, you okay?"

"Yeah, great, thanks," I said, and kept walking.

"I know you hate confrontation," she whispered to me. "We all think that was totally brave of you, how you handled that, with Chase, just now. We're the ones who made him apologize to you."

"Thanks," I said, slightly confused, slightly intrigued I admit, slightly wondering: Is this the beginning of her apology to me? "I appreciate that."

"Listen," Ava whispered, pulling me closer. "Do you want a ride home? My mom's picking us up. You know how she is about weather! You don't want to scoot home in this."

"I rode my bike."

"You *did*?"

"Yeah. But I think I'll leave it here."

"So you want a ride?" Ava asked.

I glanced at Holly. She shrugged, like whatever, maybe better than walking home in a hurricane, though, barely.

"You don't think she'd mind taking me and Holly to my house?"

"Holly?" Ava asked, as if she had no idea who I was talking about.

"Yeah," I said.

Ava leaned closer, her face in my hair. "I'm just not sure there'll be room. You know, with the Squad in there, and honestly, they like you but . . ."

"Okay," I said.

"Great," Ava said, and smiled apologetically at Holly. "Sorry, Holly."

"No," I said. "I mean, we're okay, then, walking home. It'll be fun."

Ava raised one eyebrow, the look that sends icicles through my forehead. "Suit yourself."

"Good advice," I said.

She sped up down the stairs, calling to Britney up ahead.

"You okay?" Holly said.

I let my breath out. I wanted to say, *Are you kidding? I'm awesome!* But in fact there was a pit in my stomach, watching the strawberry-blonde ponytail of my (I guess ex) best friend get farther away. Though: no icicles. So maybe that's progress?

"It's not as easy as with Chase," Holly said. "You were best friends a long time."

I nodded.

We pushed out the door. It was hard to see, with the rain coming at us sideways and sticks blowing past. Holly flipped the hood of her sweatshirt up. I yanked my hair back in a ponytail. Like for a fight?

"Wow, this storm is not kidding!" Holly yelled over the roar of the rain.

"We'll be fine!" I hollered.

"Is the universe telling us to get a ride?" she asked.

"The universe is daring us to be brave!"

"HAVE AT US, UNIVERSE!" Holly agreed.

"YOU CAN'T SCARE US, UNIVERSE!" I yelled, and then added, "PERSPECTIVE!"

"YEAH!" Holly shouted, then turned to me. "Perspective?"

"YEAH!"

"YEAH!"

We had gotten almost down the hill, still on school property, clinging to each other and laughing, when we caught up with Nadine and Beth.

"Yikes!" Beth yelled. "This is utterly bonkers! We're gonna die!"

"Not today," I told her.

Holly laughed. "Good plan!"

We were all soaked through, squinting in the teeming rain and raging wind. "Hey, do you guys want to come over?" I asked. "I live pretty close."

They couldn't hear me so I had to yell it a few more times. They both said yes, though Beth said she'd have to check in with her dad when we got there. Her phone had already died and the rest of us agreed it didn't make any sense to take out our phones. We'd just push on through and get to my house, and then call all the parents to let them know we were safe.

A stick whipped a few inches from my face. I jumped. They all shrieked and asked if I was okay. "I'm great," I said, and I meant it. I was completely soaked and a little scared of getting struck by lightning and killed, but I wasn't worried about being weird or how awful my hair looked, so, on balance, I was actually great.

"Let's hang on to one another's backpacks," I suggested. "We won't lose anybody, that way. Okay?"

They all agreed, and the four of us made a train, hands on backpacks, leaning forward into the storm. "Okay, okay," I started shout-singing. My friends, behind me, joined in.

A car was beeping beside us.

"Who's that?" Beth asked.

I don't think I've ever been that wet even in the shower. My glasses were in my backpack and everything looked like an impressionist painting to me.

But then I heard Ava's mom Samantha's voice yelling, "Get in! Girls! Hurry up!"

The back door of their SUV opened. We glanced at one another, but when the lightning lit us all up and the thunder boomed, we piled into the empty back seat of the truck.

"Thanks!" I said to Samantha.

"It's crazytown out! What were you thinking, you bananas!"

"Where's the Squad?" Holly asked Ava, who was in the front seat, staring straight ahead.

"Meeting me at my house," she said.

"Are we having a hurricane party?" Samantha asked. "What a great idea. Do you girls want to come over too? We have a generator, so even if the power goes out, you can still watch your movies or whatever you want to do. Niki, you haven't seen Ava's room since we finished painting and redecorating it!"

"Oh, thank you so much," Holly said. "But we have plans to go to Niki's already. Is that okay?"

"Oh," Samantha said, glancing at Ava, whose face was turned away.

"Do you mind dropping us at my house, Samantha?" I asked.

"Don't mind at all," she said. "This is why we have this beast. You kids have no idea how much your parents are probably going nuts right now with worry about where you are. It's not safe out."

The rain pounded so hard on the windshield as Samantha drove, I could see a flash of the road, then just wet, as the windshield wipers metronomed *not safe not safe not safe*. I sat back and closed my eyes.

"Yikes!" Samantha yelled. "Somebody build an ark!"

She was trying to sound cheery, but for once she had both hands on the wheel and was gripping it, hard.

An ark.

I looked over at Holly. "An ark," I whispered. "That is what we need."

She grabbed my hand, and, with her other hand, grabbed Nadine's. Nadine grabbed Beth's just as we skidded a little on the road. "Whoa," Sam said, recovering.

"You okay?" I asked.

"Fine," Sam said. "It's just so flooded already!"

She took a deep breath and kept going, even slower.

The dirt road to my house was basically a mud puddle. Their street, Ocean Way, is fully paved. "You can just leave us off here," I said.

"Don't be silly," Sam said. "The beast can get through any weather."

She drove slowly, leaning forward.

As we pulled into the driveway, I saw Mom's bright blue car with the lights on, in the flashes of clear as the wipers swiped uselessly at the windshield.

# 42

MOM JUMPED OUT of her car. "Niki! I was texting and calling you!" she yelled.

"I'm sorry," I said. "I forgot I had turned my phone off and then we—"

"I was so scared you were in a ditch on the side of the road or hit by lightning on that stupid bike, or . . ."

"Mom!" She was soaked and yelling our family business in front of everyone, and maybe crying, I don't know. Her mascara was running down her cheeks.

"And my stupid car won't start and, oh, Niki, I'm so glad you're okay."

She grabbed me into a hug.

"I mean, it's okay if you're not okay," she whispered through my wet hair. "I just want you to be a little okay, sorry."

"Mom, it's okay. I'm fine."

She held my wet face for a second with her strong, wet hands, then let go and waved at Samantha.

Samantha opened her window, despite the teeming rain, and Mom ran over to her, saying *thank you* and *sorry*. Samantha, her hair and mascara ruined too, was answering, *no* and *of course* and *you were completely right, I'm so sorry, I never meant*...

And then they were hugging, awkwardly, through the open window.

Ava was still looking out the opposite way, away from me.

Mom waved as Sam backed out of our driveway and pulled away, then turned to look at bedraggled us, standing dripping on our porch. I looked at us too. We were definitely not a fashionable crew. I turned back to Mom, steeling myself for the forced smile to hide judgment on them, on me.

Instead, when she got up onto the porch, she sniffled, pushed her stringy hair off her face, and said, "Hi, girls," with a giggle in her voice. "Nice weather, huh?"

"Smiles, sunshine, and a quick cleanup make everything better," Holly said.

"Wow," Mom said. "That's what my mom always said! I don't know. I'm starting to find that expression kind of annoying and fake, you know? Maybe you also need a few towels, to make things better."

"Sounds good to me!" Nadine said.

"Good, better, best," I said as we all walked in.

"Ugh," Mom said. "Let's let it rest!"

"Okay," I said. "Rest sounds good."

"Doesn't it?" Mom asked. "Niki, come help me get towels for everybody."

I followed her to the linen closet while my friends tried to peel off their jackets and boots in the mudroom. Mom grabbed fluffy towels from the shelf where they were all rolled neatly, and loaded them into my arms. "Thanks," I said. "This is perfect. I hope it's okay that I brought everybody. . . ."

"Listen to me," she whispered. "I want you to know this: You don't have to be perfect, and you don't have to seem perfect. I'm not. Daddy's not. Danny's not. We're all very not. I like things to look nice. It's not because I want to hide reality. It's because, well, it calms me down and makes me happy, when things look pretty. It's not that I'm ashamed of what's underneath. I love what's underneath. We're all perfectly imperfect and if anybody is judgy about any of us, well, that's on them. They can just keep that all the way to themselves. I think you're . . ."

"A soaking mess?" I didn't want her to say she thought I was *the finest kind*. *The finest kind* is too much to live up to.

"Well," Mom said. "An *awesome* soaking mess. How's that?"

"Okay," I said. "Great, actually."

"Ava didn't want to join you?"

I took a deep breath. "Ava's going through some stuff lately," I said.

"Aren't we all," Mom said.

I looked her in the eye. I nodded a little. She nodded too.

She tucked my hair behind my ear, then gave me a kiss on my forehead. "Why don't you give those out. Should I make some hot chocolate?"

"That would be great," I said.

"Good."

Dad rushed in from the family room while we were all toweling off. "You're home."

"Ayuh," I said.

"Did you have fun?"

"We did," I said, realizing it was true.

"Good, because you're never leaving the house again."

"Dad," I said.

He held out his arms for a hug. I leaned my head against his chest and felt him close around me, all fleece and warmth.

"Oooo, I should text my parents," Nadine said.

"Me too," said Beth.

"Me three," said Holly.

"Absolutely," Dad said. The thunder kaboomed and we all, except Dad, jumped.

"Yikes!" Beth yelled.

"Right?" He opened his arms and let me go. "And you girls were all out there in it. How do you think your parents feel, hearing that wind and rain and all?"

"My phone died," Beth said meekly.

"You wanna know the parents' prayer?" Dad asked, running his hand through his thinning hair. "It's all of four letters long. BE OK. That's it. That's all we really want, at the end of the day. We breathe it in and breathe it out every second since you stinkers are born. BE OK. BE OK. That'll be enough. Be OK."

"Dad!"

Dad looked up at the ceiling and blinked a few times. Nadine put her hand over her heart.

"Who's hungry?" Dad asked, extra loud.

"Do you have ramekins?" Holly asked.

"I think I might," Dad said, and cleared his throat. "Come look with me. After you call your parents. All of you! Niki, check your phone, huh? I think it's off?"

"It is," I said, fishing it out of my bag and powering it up. "Beth, you wanna use mine?" A ton of texts crowded my screen. I got rid of them so she could text her dad.

"Do it now," Dad said, on his way to the kitchen. "Right now!"

"Your dad is such a moosh," Nadine whispered to me. "I adore him."

"Your family is so great," Beth said, looking up from texting on my phone. "Oh, my dad says it's fine I'm here and he's glad I'm safe. What's with the dads, today?"

"Barometric pressure affects dads a lot, maybe," Nadine said. "Got the okay from my parents too. They're putting masking tape on the windows, for some reason."

"Oh, mine do that too, in storms," Beth said.

"Wanna see my room?" I asked them, taking my phone back from Beth. "It might be a mess, but you can plug in your phone and use the bathroom or whatever you want."

"Great, thanks," Beth said. On the way up, we passed Danny's motto poster. "Be clam?" she asked.

"Family goals," I said.

Danny was in his room, not playing a game but digging through his closet. He poked his head out and smiled at me.

"Niki," he said. "I'm glad you didn't get hit by lightning and die."

"Me too," I said. "This is Danny, my brother."

Nadine and Beth said hi to him, but Danny was still looking right at me. "If you died, it would break my heart."

"Awww," Beth said. "You're the nicest brother! I bet my brother would be psyched if I got hit by lightning."

"You might be wrong," Danny said. "It's hard to know what other people are feeling. You have to watch their body language."

"So true," Beth said. "Thanks, Danny."

"But maybe you and your brother aren't as close as me and Niki. We're best friends."

"That is the sweetest thing I've ever heard," Nadine said.

"I have excellent hearing," Danny said. "But also I get headaches with big changes in barometric pressure, so I stayed home from school today."

"Do you still have a headache?" Beth asked. Which was so nice. Instead of being like, what the heck kind of conversational shift is *that*, they just went with it.

"No," he said. "My eyes are sensitive to light. I might be

on the spectrum. So I might get a life coach for help with organization and social skills. Also, I was in the newspaper."

"Yeah, Danny, what?" I said. "You were? I just heard about that!"

"Me too. Boone sent me a link yesterday. Boone is my best friend in school. Niki is my best friend in the world."

"That's so cool, that you were in the newspaper," Beth said. "For what?"

"The garbage collectors came to my birthday party. The newspaper found out about it and they asked if we had any pictures and if we gave permission for them to write a story about it. They thought I might be embarrassed because none of the kids in my grade except Boone came to my party, but I wasn't embarrassed. I only gave out some of the invitations, not all of them."

"You *what?*" I asked.

"A lot of the kids in my grade don't like me, so why would I want them at my birthday? A birthday party is to celebrate that the person was born. Boone is happy I was born. And some of the other kids might be, but they didn't come, so I guess not. The garbage guys are happy I was born. One of them is afraid I will beat him up, but I never would."

"So, it got into the newspaper?" Holly asked, behind us in the hall.

"Yes," Danny said. "I'm famous now. And so is Niki, because it says 'photo credit, Niki Ames' in very small print under the picture she took of me with my friends the garbage guys. But she is not as famous as I am." He smiled huge. "Mom sent it to the paper, but she didn't know if they'd print it. She's proud I'm famous, and also that Niki is, but less than me."

"That's awesome, Danny," Holly said.

"Yes," Danny said. "Boone is putting it in a frame to give me as a present, even though he already gave me another present, which was a game. Now I have to look for flashlights, in case we lose power in the storm."

He turned around and went back into his room, where his DANNY balloons were bobbling near his window. "I like your balloons," Beth called after him. "Those are the best kind."

"They don't pop!" Danny yelled back.

"I know, that other kind makes me so anxious," Beth said. "I keep waiting for the BOOM. Plus, these last longer."

"I know," Danny said. "Until they get wrinkly and low and then Niki stabs them with a knife."

"You brute!" Nadine yelled at me.

Danny laughed. "You brute!" he echoed.

"I'm a monster, I know," I admitted as we went into my room. "I didn't realize he knew I stabbed his balloons last year," I whispered. "I thought I was so stealth. Anyway, that's Danny." I plugged my phone in.

"He's adorable," Beth said.

"Yeah," I said, "he is, right? I mean, he's not your average . . ."

"Exactly!" Holly said. "Unique in all the world, and completely at home in his own self."

I nodded. "I could learn a lot from him."

"Seriously, who couldn't," Nadine' said. "Well, from everybody, right?"

"Ms. Andry, especially," Holly said. "How goals is she? She just has no use for anyone's nonsense. I love her."

"Same," I said.

We sat on my floor and started discussing which teachers were goals and which were pitfalls, when Beth's phone revived itself and started buzzing nonstop.

We all checked our phones, sitting on my floor in comfortable, if still slightly damp, silence.

I had missed a series of texts from Isabel:

**Hey me and Britney and Madeleine are at Scoops with Kallista and my cousin Rhys, who is your biggest fan**

**We're boarding up the windows so they don't get smashed in the storm**

**Just finished so now as a prize guess what we're eating**

**Niki Specials—so good!**

**Bet you know what that is, right?**

**OMG best thing we've ever eaten, Madeleine is moaning with happiness**

**Kallista wants to know if it's okay with you if we make you famous and call them that officially?**

**The Niki Special—on the sign at Scoops! You've hit the BIG TIME!**

I glanced over at Nadine and Beth, who were done with their phones and had moved on to looking at my bookcase, fangirling over all my favorites, calling out one title after another and shrieking at how good that one was, or this one.

I quickly texted back to Isabel:

**That is the sweetest and being famous would be amazing not gonna lie it's my secret life goal but honestly would it be okay if we call it the Rhys Special? He is the genius behind it, after all.**

She texted back a string of hearts, and then:

**Isabel: Did you hear what Milo said to Chase? I don't know if he's in love with you or just a really good guy, but—swooooon.**

I was texting her a bunch of **???**s when another text came in.

**Milo: Did you make it home in the hurricane?**

**I saw your bike still there when we left but Robby said you already left**

**Sorry to text again but we waited awhile to see if you were there but**

**me: Yeah, home safe and sound**

**Milo: Phew**

Should I ask him what he said to Chase?

**How about you and Robby?** I responded instead, like we were polite pretend-adults. **Safe and sound?**

**Milo: Well, Robby is good he didn't skid off the road**

**WHAT**, I texted back quickly

"You okay?" Holly asked me. "Your face has gone through pretty much every emotion in the past forty-five seconds."

I laughed. "I think Milo might have gotten into a bike accident. He's—hang on."

"Don't they live next door to you?" Beth asked.

"Cocoa!" Mom called from the kitchen. "And Dad found the ramekins!"

"Okay!" I yelled back.

**Left bits of my right eyebrow on Victory, but other than that, I should be okay**, Milo texted.

"Something disgusting?" Holly asked.

"Yeah," I said. "Is my face that obvious a window into my feelings?"

All three of them nodded. "You're the most expressive person," Holly said. "It's kind of the thing about you."

"*That's* the thing about me?"

"That you have big, deep, very obvious soul-shaking feelings?" Holly said. "Yeah, kind of."

"I thought I was invisible and mysterious!"

They all cracked up.

"Or at least blurry."

"Nope, you're completely specific," Nadine said.

"So is Milo okay?" Beth asked.

"Scraped up, sounds like," I said. "His face, maybe?"

"Ew!" Beth said.

"Yikes," said Nadine. "His face?"

"His eyebrow, he said." I tried not to frown.

"Maybe I'll finally be able to tell them apart," Beth said.

"That would be a benefit," Nadine said.

"Niki can tell them apart," Holly said. They both looked at me for confirmation. "To be fair she lives next door, so . . ."

We started heading downstairs to the kitchen.

"Or maybe he got in a fistfight with Chase," Nadine said on our way. "They sure were arguing, under the We Are All Friends sign, right?"

"We must've just missed that," Holly said.

"I don't think Milo would be in a fistfight," Beth said. "You don't think Chase punched him and he's just making up a bike accident to cover, do you?"

"Why was he fighting with Chase?" I asked.

They all smiled at me like, *Really?*

"What?"

"Because of what Chase . . ." Beth started.

"How he kissed you without your permission," Nadine said. "Milo was really calling him some choice names. That was Milo, right? It might've been Robby."

Holly nodded. "I guarantee it was Milo."

"He did?" I asked. "Aren't he and Robby, like, best friends with Chase?"

"I guess not anymore," Beth said.

Holly turned to me. "Maybe you should see if they want to come over to make molten chocolate cakes."

"Yeah?" I said.

She shrugged. "Don't you want to?"

I smiled a bit. "Sort of?"

"Then you should!"

Mom had set out mugs of cocoa for all of us. "Thanks," I said. "Hey, is it okay if I invite Milo and Robby over too?"

"Of course," Mom said. "There's room for everyone!"

"I like this ark better than the other kind," Holly said. "Don't you?"

"So much better," I said, hugging the warm mug between my chilled hands.

# 43

MILO'S RIGHT EYE was a bit bruised and swollen, and a shallow cut sliced his eyebrow.

"Looks worse than it feels," he assured my mom.

"Looks like Niki's elephant," Holly said.

"An elephant?" Robby asked, then turned to his brother. "Dude, she said you look like an elephant."

"The elephant in the room," Holly said.

"I don't see it," Beth said, assessing it critically, as if maybe if she tilted her head at some specific angle she'd see how Milo looked like an elephant.

The wind rattled our windows.

"To be fair," I said, "my elephant bowl doesn't look much like an elephant either. But he does have a golden scar."

"Cool," Milo said. "An elephant with a golden scar? I've never seen one like that."

"He's unique!" I said. "A little fragile, turns out."

"Same, same," Milo said. "Turns out."

"Milo!" Danny yelled from the family room.

"Coming!" He turned to me. "Come see. We're building the most massive awesome parking garage for garbage trucks in history!"

"Amazing," I said, but grabbed his elbow as he walked toward the family room, where everybody else was chatting and laughing with my brother. We were alone in the front hall. "Hey," I asked him. "Did something happen between you and Chase today?"

"I know you don't need anyone standing up for you," Milo said, looking down at his socks. "I just added my opinion to yours. Chase was kind of smirking in the lobby when I got down the stairs, and maybe he was just trying to hide his shame, but you know what? He should be ashamed. He should stew in his shame and suffer."

"Milo."

He looked up at me. "I would never kiss you without asking first."

How does a normal human exist on the speeding, spinning planet without falling off? "I know," I whispered.

"At some point I'm gonna ask you permission. When I get my courage together."

"Okay," I somehow managed.

"Maybe when my face looks better," he said. "Increase my odds of getting a yes."

"Your face is good," I whispered.

"It's kind of a bashed-up mess right now."

"Not to me," I said.

"Really?"

"I like it," I whispered.

"I like yours, too," he whispered back.

"MILO!" Danny yelled.

"Coming," Milo answered, and gave me his lopsided smile. And then, as he walked away, toward the family room, he touched the back of his hand to the underneath of my chin, just for one second, maybe two.

I leaned against the doorframe for a minute.

My excellent chin.

*He likes me. Right? He's choosing me. And I'm choosing him.*

*Best feeling in the whole world.*

I stood at the edge of the family room and admired what my brother and my friends had created, with blocks and tracks and trucks. Danny looked happier than he had in so long. *Can a heart break through your ribs from pounding so hard?*

*Asking for a friend, a family room full of my friends.*

*A friends room full of family.*

Branches clattered against the windows, and lightning flickered like a strobe.

"Get ready for chocolate cakes to die for!" Holly yelled from the kitchen. "Niki, come see!"

That's when all the lights went out.

"Uh-oh," Dad said in the sudden darkness.

"Ouch!" Milo yelled.

"Everybody stay still!" Mom yelled. Lightning lit the room, and thunder boomed right after.

"Don't worry!" Danny yelled. "I got all the candles and the flashlights! They're in this bag!"

"Hooray for Danny!" Beth yelled.

Danny flicked on a flashlight and shined it in my eyes.

"Danny," I said. "You're the MVP of the day."

"Your favorite person other than me said to gather flashlights and candles," Danny said.

"Your favorite?" Milo asked.

"Breezy Khan," Danny said.

"I love her!" Milo yelled.

Robby flicked on the flashlight Danny handed to him. "He does," Robby said. "Milo is in love with Breezy Khan."

Milo blushed.

"Who isn't?" Nadine said. "You need calm winds to brew a hurricane."

"Yes," I agreed. "Severe clear."

"See?" Milo said, knocking his brother over. "Everybody thinks she's awesome."

"You're all freaks," Robby said.

"True that," Nadine agreed.

Robby threw a couch pillow at her, which she caught and threw back.

I glanced at Mom, who was in the doorway. She shrugged. "It *is* a throw pillow," she said.

"The molten cakes are extra, well, molty!" Holly yelled from the kitchen. "But come try them!"

On my way, my phone buzzed in my pocket.

Ava.

"Be right there," I told everyone. I grabbed a lit candle and went to the bathroom, locking the door behind me.

**Ava: Niki you have to come over**

**me: Why?**

**Ava: My mom will come get you**

**Come**

**I need you**

**me: What's going on?**

**Ava: Okay if I tell her to come get you?**

**me: Ava what's going on?**

**Ava: Did you lose power?**

**me: Yeah**

**Ava: Us too—but we have a generator. So you should fully come**

**me: You know I have people here**

**Ava: Fine fine bring Holly if you want but honestly, Nadine and Beth? Dude.**

**me: Is something wrong?**

I looked at myself in the mirror while I waited for her response. My hair was huge, the way Ava says is a scary mess. I decided to try to see myself gently instead. I tried. Deep breath. Maybe it looks like a lion's mane.

Maybe it was the soft candlelight. But I didn't look like a disaster to myself.

My face is liked. Milo likes it. Maybe I could find a way to see even myself gently? *I'm a lion*, I whispered to myself. *Not an abandoned elephant.*

*Independent. And surrounded by friends.*

A big chunk of text came through from Ava:

**Okay, here's the thing and I did not want to tell you this because whatever you might think, I really am your best friend. I would never want you to be hurt. Okay: I was just at Isabel's with the Squad and all the boys are there, you know, for hurricane party . . .**

**Wait**, I texted. **You were at Isabel's? JUST NOW?**

**Ava: YES, KEEP UP. We were having a party at Isabel's (don't be mad you weren't invited/I didn't want to say anything at school in front of Holly—you know I love you but tbf you left the last one in a rude hurry, right? Even though now I understand why and you were right. I convinced everybody you weren't being a drama queen and we're all fully on your side. But it's not like they'd want Holly there, no offense). Anyway Chase was saying all kinds of nasty crap about you and turning everybody against you including Milo who**

**MILO?** I texted.

**Ava: I know you like him, Niki. You told me Saturday, remember? I was trying to speak up for you to him but**

**me: He's at Isabel's? Now? Are you there?**

**Ava: No, I told you, I left. I'm home. I know we're taking a break but the truth is I miss you and I can say things to you, brutal truths bc we're best friends forever. But other people talking about you behind your back? No.**

**Milo is here**, I texted her.

No response.

I opened the door and went down the steps, my belly in a knot. Everybody was in the kitchen, eating molten chocolate cake by candlelight. "You okay?" Mom asked me.

"I—Milo?"

He looked up at me and smiled a little. His cut across his eyebrow looked so cute, my knees went way more molten than what he had in his spoon.

"Were you at Isabel's?"

"Yeah," he said.

"Oh." I checked my phone. Still nothing back from Ava.

"Remember?" he asked. "We talked about soda making our eyes cry?"

"Today, I mean," I said.

"Oh. Nope," he answered. "School, ditch, home, here. Kind of a full day, honestly." He blushed a little, which made me blush too.

I looked at Robby.

"Same," he said. "Except the ditch, because I actually know how to ride a bike."

Milo shoved Robby.

I took a picture of my friends at my kitchen table, with the dark storm raging outside the kitchen window. I sent it to Ava without any words.

I watch the three dots flicker, disappear, flicker again, disappear again.

**Can I call you?** Ava finally texted. I texted her a thumbs-up.

"Be right back," I said out loud.

Milo glanced up from his ramekin. He looked even more concerned than usual. Maybe it was because of that eyebrow. I smiled at him without even meaning to. It felt like when you tip your face up to the sky on the first sunny day of spring. He smiled back just the same way.

"You okay?" Mom asked as I dashed up the steps, heart pounding but in a good way.

"I am," I answered.

# 44

I ANSWERED ON the first ring, despite my plan to wait for the second.

"Niki?" Her voice was shaky.

"Yeah."

"I'm the worst. I know I am. You don't have to say it; I know you know."

"Ava."

"I'm a terrible best friend. I know. You're the only person who sticks with me, who doesn't give up on me, and I know I don't deserve you. I get that."

"Why did you lie to me?" I asked. "Why did you tell me Milo was at a party with you, when—"

"Because I'm here alone, Niki! Even my mom's not talking to me, because apparently your mom turned her against me, told her I've been horrible to you or some crap like that. And you turned my friends against me. I'm not mad. You had every right to. And I get it, about Chase. Okay? What you were pissed at him about but also how I, whatever, fell short. Was a bad friend to you. I was jealous. That's the truth, the simple truth. You know I get jealous—but, Niki, admit it: you kissed the boy I liked. Whether you wanted to or not, he kissed you. Of course I was jealous. But I'm the worst, fine."

"You sure think about yourself a lot," I said.

"What?" she asked.

"You were in the middle of apologizing, or were you?"

"Niki, I just said I was sorry, like, a hundred times."

"I'm not sure you said it even once, actually," I said. "You should have, because you actually have been pretty terrible to me lately. But then you got distracted by yourself and suddenly you're the *worst*, which, obviously you're not *the worst*, so it turns into me having to tell you you're fine, we're fine, you shouldn't be so hard on yourself, you know I love you. Why do you do that?"

"You're making me feel terrible, Niki."

"No, I'm not," I told her. "Maybe you're just feeling terrible, and it's not my fault, Ava."

I heard her crying on the other end. Almost everything in my brain was yelling at me to comfort her, say never mind, tell her everything's fine and she should come over or I'd come there and we're good.

Only one tiny instinct in me disagreed, quietly insistent, and it sounded like:

*I DON'T WANT YOU.*

I didn't have to yell it to know it. No eraser could delete the truth of it.

*I don't want you.* It felt like a calm wind in my stormy soul. I didn't want to be friends with Ava.

I was thinking about Danny's silver balloons. How you have to stick a knife into them, eventually, when they deflate so much they're just sad, hovering inches above the floor. It's time for them to go. They don't pop. They just sigh like *whatever* when you eventually stab them to death.

"Tell me what you want me to do," Ava was whispering. "I'll do whatever you want, okay? Just tell me; don't just sit there all stony silent. What do you want me to say? I'm sorry? I said it. I'm sorry! You want me to say it a thousand times? Sorry sorry sorry sorry—"

"Stop."

"Fine, then. What do you want me to do, be more like Holly, nod at everything anyone says? Fine. I'll change. Okay?"

"You can't change who you are," I said. "I would never ask you to do that. Only a bad friend would ask that. Why do you always try to make me feel bad, Ava?"

"I don't!"

I heard a burst of laughter, from downstairs. Danny's high cackle harmonized right into the sound.

"I gotta go," I said to Ava.

"Oh, Niki," Ava said. "Don't be like that."

"Me?" I asked. "I'm the finest kind."

I hung up the phone and tossed it onto my bed. Fumble wagged his tail like *yes yes yes* and followed me down to be with my friends.

RACHEL VAIL is the award-winning author of more than forty books for young people. Her most recent novels are *Well, That Was Awkward* and *Unfriended* for young teens, and the Justin Case trilogy for kids. She has a new chapter-book series just coming out, starring Justin's feisty little sister: A Is for Elizabeth. Her picture books include *Piggy Bunny* and *Sometimes I'm Bombaloo*. Rachel lives in New York City with her husband, their two sons, and a tortoise named Lightning. She grew up in New Rochelle, New York, with her parents and her younger brother, Jon. Among other awesome qualities, Jon is on the autism spectrum, and was Rachel's first reader, audience, and booster. He taught her to tell stories by listening so intently to them, and also that each person has a unique perspective and way of navigating the world. Rachel would probably never have been a writer without Jon. She continues to learn from him, to root for him, and to be proud of him.

You can visit Rachel online at RachelVail.com.